What Readers Are Saying about Forbidden

"Nothing I have seen provides better spiritual equipment for today's youth to fi—
spiritual battle ragi—
Myers's Forbidden
family should have

C. Pet—
Presid—

"During the past 18 y——— my husband and I have been involved in youth ministry, we have seen a definite need for these books. Bill fills the need with comedy, romance, action, and riveting suspense with clear teaching. It's a nonstop page-turner!"

Robin Jones Gunn
Author, Christy Miller series

"Bill Myers's books will help equip families. It's interesting, too, that the Sunday school curriculum market, for which I write, is examining topics such as reincarnation and out-of-body experiences. The Forbidden Doors books are timely."

Carla Williams
Mother and freelance writer

"Fast-moving, exciting, and loaded with straightforward answers to tough questions, Forbidden Doors is Bill Myers at his best."

Jon Henderson
Author

The Forbidden Doors series

FORBIDDEN ● DOORS

the scream

JAMES RIORDAN

Based on the Forbidden Doors series created by Bill Myers

 Tyndale House Publishers, Inc.   Wheaton, Illinois

Published in association with the literary agency of Alive
Communications, Inc., 7680 Goddard Street, Suite 200,
Colorado Springs, CO 80920.

ISBN 0-8423-5741-6, mass paper

Printed in the United States of America

07 06 05 04
6   5   4   3   2

For George Lord,
a friend in good times
and bad

If you need wisdom—if you want to know what God wants you to do—ask him, and he will gladly tell you.

James 1:5

1

At the Poseidon
Arena in San Francisco, the mega-popular
heavy metal band The Scream tore through
their last set in front of a packed house. The
music was loud and the show was exciting—
a combination of the latest high-tech special
effects, makeup, and costumes.

The Scream's lead singer, Tommy Doland,
had a red pentagram painted across his face.

His intense dark eyes peered out from the center. His shoulder-length hair was coal black, except for a great shock of bright blue hair in the front. His outfit was part Roman emperor and part Darth Vader. His long cape billowed out behind while he strutted the length of the stage singing:

I'm riding on wings of fire.
I'm burning the fields of desire.
In touch with the overlord,
He takes me higher. . . .

On the word *higher* his voice catapulted into a loud shriek, one of the band's trademarks. The audience's response was immediate and frenzied.

The audience itself was something to behold. Dressed in homemade versions of the same costumes and makeup as the band members, the crowd seemed even angrier than the band. They moved constantly, slamming into each other with a fierceness that was somewhere between a wild, uncontrolled dance and an outright riot.

Mike Parsek, the drummer of The Scream, looked toward the angry wave of humanity as he hammered out the driving beat and wondered just how close the crowd was to losing control. Three kids had been hospitalized last week at their concert in Denver. Mike was the first to admit that it could've been a lot worse. Kids had been crushed to death at other bands' concerts. Even so, creating that kind of excitement was the key element of the band's performance. After all, the fans came because they *wanted* a wild ride.

Mike scanned the screaming fans again and frowned. Sometimes he worried how that ride might end.

Tommy Doland never seemed worried about that part of the concert. His method of operation was always the same: Take it higher, drive it harder, push it farther.

A highlight of the show was always Mike's drum solo. No matter how much Mike pushed it, Doland always wanted to go a little farther. For this tour the drum solo had become a big production number loaded with special effects. The climax of the solo now included the eruption of a giant fire cannon that had been made to look like a fierce dragon. When Mike's solo reached its peak, two huge flamethrowers concealed in the dragon's mechanical throat blasted out twenty-foot streaks of fire over the heads of the audience, making them scream in delight.

It was time for Mike's solo, and he jumped in with a vengeance. As he increased the volume and tempo, he felt the tension build in the audience—who expected something spectacular at this point—and in himself, as he prepared for the coming explosion.

Launching into the final pattern, Mike eyed stage manager Billy Phelps, whose job it was to ignite the cannon. As usual, Billy nodded along with the beat, one finger on the button, ready to fire. Mike steeled himself for the blast and nodded slightly, but the visual cue was unnecessary. Billy knew the timing by heart. He pressed the button.

There was a brief hesitation and then a crackling sound that Mike had never heard before. A puff of smoke came from the dragon's mouth. This was followed by a clinking sound that came off like a groan from the pit of the dragon's stomach, which was then followed by silence.

Something was wrong.

Mike breathed a sigh of relief. Part of him was glad it hadn't worked. Every time the cannon went off, he wondered if the teens in the first row were going to become burnt offerings. Then, out of the corner of his eye, Mike caught a glimpse of Tommy Doland. The lead singer appeared to be laughing.

~

Later on in the show, the band wailed away as Doland sang the lead to their latest hit, "Army of the Night." Meanwhile, Billy worked on the broken dragon.

"I can't figure out why this thing isn't firing," he muttered to himself as he examined the circuitry of the control panel for the fire cannon. "Everything here looks OK. Must be up in the barrel. Better cut the power."

With that, he switched off the control board and began crawling underneath the cannon. Onstage Doland sang:

Army of the night,
Not afraid to fight,
Marching into danger
Without any light.

As Doland writhed across the stage, the crowd screamed. Guitarist Jackie Vee ripped into a searing solo. Meanwhile, Billy had worked his way to the end of the cannon's barrel.

Doland continued singing:

Army of the night,
The master's wishes soar,
Risking our life
To fight an unholy war.

At these words, as though an unseen hand moved it, the ignition switch on the cannon's control panel vibrated to the on position. Unaware of this, Billy reached inside the

5

barrel to shine his flashlight down the dragon's mouth. Doland continued to sing:

Army of the night,
Unholy alliance,
Our soul submitted
For your compliance.

Suddenly, the loading mechanism of the fire cannon began to shake, but since Billy was at the opposite end, he didn't notice.

Mike looked up from the drums, sensing a difference in the cannon's vibration. He looked over to the control panel and saw that it had switched on. Then, with horror, he saw the small red light on the loading mechanism also flicker.

The cannon was about to fire!

Mike tried to catch Billy's eye, but the stage manager leaned down so far into the cannon that only his legs could be seen.

"Billy!" Mike shouted. "Get out of there!"

Billy didn't hear him. The loading mechanism vibrated, and the light on the panel shifted from red to green.

Mike knew that he would never reach Billy in time, so he hurled one of his drumsticks at the stage manager's legs. It connected, and a bewildered Billy pulled his head out from the cannon to see what was happening. Spotting the stick on the floor, he looked over to

Mike, who waved frantically for him to get out of the way.

But there was no time. The cannon fired.

The flame that shot from the dragon's head was a wall of fire. It shot over Billy's head and out across the stage. Grant Simone, the band's bass player, turned just in time to see his amplifier catch fire. With a yelp, he dived out of the way.

Billy was not so lucky. His clothes were aflame.

The crowd screamed, unsure if this was part of the show or an accident. Mike leaped off his drum riser and ran toward Billy. As he passed Doland, he snatched the lead singer's cape and charged for the burning man. Leaping through the air, Mike landed on top of Billy and knocked him to the ground. Quickly he began to smother the fire with the cape.

After several long, terrifying seconds, it was over.

Thirty minutes later Billy was carried off in an ambulance. Another fifteen minutes passed before the police had cleared the auditorium completely.

Onstage the road crew began to break down the elaborate set. Mike, still stunned, stood by his drums watching one of the roadies begin to dismantle the huge fire cannon.

"Hey, Mike," the roadie said, "why didn't Billy shut that thing down while he worked on it? Doesn't he know better than that?"

Mike looked at the roadie for a long moment. "He *did* shut it down. I saw him do it. The thing . . . kicked on by itself."

The roadie looked at Mike as if he were nuts but didn't say anything.

Mike left the stage and headed for Doland's dressing room. He knocked twice on the door.

"Come in," Doland said.

Mike opened the door to see Doland standing before the mirror, still wearing his stage makeup. "Oh, it's the hero of the hour. Come on in, Mike. What's up?"

"Doland, I know for a fact that Billy shut that cannon down before he started working on it. I saw him do it. The thing came on by itself like some sort of . . ." He trailed off, not sure what to say.

Doland smiled strangely. "Some sort of what, Mike?"

"Some sort of . . . monster. Like it had a mind of its own."

Doland laughed gruffly. "Come now, Mikey. A church boy like you doesn't buy into that sort of nonsense, does he? Sounds like black magic, doesn't it? You don't believe in black magic now, do you?"

Mike turned away from Doland's sneer.

"I've told you before. I don't like you teasing me about my father."

Doland gave a look of mock sympathy. "Oh, you mean the good reverend? I wouldn't dream of it, Mike."

"How can you be joking around like this with Billy in the hospital?"

Doland shrugged. "Billy's going to be all right. You heard the paramedic. He'll be OK, thanks to that quick business you did with my cape—which, by the way, you owe me for."

Mike couldn't believe his ears. "You're worried about the cost of the cape?"

Doland shook his head. "Not really. I know that what happened here tonight is good for business. This little accident will sell a hundred thousand more CDs for us by the end of the week."

"It's not about money, Doland. It's like I've been saying all along. Things are out of hand. This devil stuff has gone too far."

Doland squinted his eyes and mimicked Mike's voice. *"This devil stuff?* Little church boy's afraid of the big bad devil stuff, eh? Sometimes I think you're in the wrong band, Mikey boy."

Mike knew he was on risky ground since Doland could easily get him kicked out of the band if he wanted to push the issue. "Listen to me for a minute," he continued. "Something has changed. Can't you see that?"

"I see far more than you, Mikey. But don't sweat it. I know what I'm doing."

Mike shook his head. This was getting him nowhere. He started to leave, then paused at the door. "It used to be fun, Tommy, but . . . don't you see? We're losing control—"

Doland cut him off with a nasty laugh. "I haven't lost control of anything, Mikey. Everything is just the way I want it."

~

It had not been one of Scott Williams's better days. . . .

First the church's youth group camping trip was canceled because they couldn't find enough chaperones.

Then Mom asked him to clean his room. Naturally, he figured that meant piling everything that was on the floor up onto his bed so he could go play baseball with the guys. That part was fine. It was coming home and finding Mom steamed that wasn't so fine. That and the discipline she had in mind for him.

"I still don't see why I have to wash these stupid windows," he complained for the tenth time.

"Because they're dirty," Mom replied.

"Why can't Becka help?"

Mom sighed, tucking a strand of brown hair currently under siege by gray behind her ear. They had had this conversation in one form or another several hundred times. "If you'd cleaned your room the way I asked you to, I wouldn't have given you this extra duty."

"You said you wanted to see the floor of my room. Well?"

"I also wanted to see your bed. Scotty, you're fifteen! You're too old to pull a stunt like that."

"OK! OK! I'm sorry," Scott mumbled as he went back to wiping the living room window. Outside he could see his older sister, Rebecca, playing football with her sort-of boyfriend, Ryan Riordan. Scott waited until Ryan lobbed her a pass before rapping on the window to distract her. "Hey, Becka!"

Becka caught the ball before turning toward her brother in the house. "Yes, Scott?" she called pleasantly. "May I help you?"

Scott grimaced, then called out, "Why don't you guys come in here and give me a hand with these windows!"

Becka laughed. "No way! You earned that job, little bro."

Scott went back to his mumbling. "Might as well clean windows. With the camping trip canceled, it's going to be another boring week. I *never* get to do *anything.*"

"What are you harping about now?" Mom asked as she walked through the room.

"Nothing," Scott answered. "I was just

wondering why we never get to do anything
fun. It's boring hanging around Crescent Bay
all the time."

Mom looked surprised. "How can you say
that? You've had quite a few adventures
since we moved to Crescent Bay a while ago.
You've also traveled all over the place. You
got to visit Louisiana not long ago. Your
sister went to Europe."

"That's different," Scott whined. "We were
helping Z."

Z was their friend from the Internet.
Although they'd never met him in person,
he'd led them into all sorts of intense adventures helping various people.

"Are you telling me that you never have
any fun on these trips?" Mom asked.

Scott shrugged. "A little, I suppose. But
Z always sends us to goofy places. Why can't
he send us someplace exciting to do something fun?"

"Let me guess—" Mom pretended to
search for an answer—"because Z isn't your
personal cruise director?"

Scott frowned but only for a second as he
suddenly saw a large FedEx truck stop in
front of their house. He raced past Mom and
headed outside, even managing to beat his
sister to the truck.

The driver laughed and handed him a
large envelope. "Sign here, son."

Scott signed the form and quickly opened the envelope.

"What is it?" Becka asked.

Scott examined the contents. "I'm not sure . . . some airline tickets, a hotel reservation, and some other kind of tickets. . . . *Wow!*"

By now Mom was out the door as well. "Wow, what?"

Scott was so excited he could hardly speak. "It's the concert tickets from Z. . . . Our trip to L.A.! It's been like a month since he mentioned it. He sent us three free tickets *and* backstage passes to see The Scream in Los Angeles. Awesome!"

"The who?" Mom asked.

"The Scream," he explained. "Remember I told you about them, Mom? They're so awesome! And we're going to get to meet them!"

Mom took the package and read the computer-generated note that accompanied the tickets. "All it says is, 'Look for the drummer. More later. Z.' Well, I can't say I'm happy about Z's wanting to send you on another mysterious trip. But I see there's a ticket for me, too," she said. "I suppose I could use a short vacation."

Scott was all smiles. "Then we can go?"

Mom nodded. "All of us can go."

"Great! Just wait'll the guys hear about this!" He turned to his sister. "Is this cool or what?"

Becka looked at him before finally managing a lame, "Yeah . . . cool."

But the feeling in her gut told her she was anything but thrilled about this. The Scream was popular with all the kids at school. But from what she'd heard of their stuff, the band was definitely heavy metal—real head-banger stuff. She didn't have a big problem with that. But the fact that they definitely flirted with satanic stuff *was* a problem. That kind of stuff always gave her the creeps. Even now she felt her skin crawl.

What possible reason could Z have for wanting them to meet The Scream?

2

$\mathcal{S}$cott lost no time in telling his friends about his upcoming trip. Already there had been at least four teens at the door, each holding a Scream CD and a photo and asking if Scott could get them autographed. Of course, Scott said it would be no problem. In fact, it seemed to Becka that with each new person he talked to, he made a bigger deal out of the L.A. trip.

Before long he had gone from a member of the audience to "a personal friend of the band."

"I never said that," Scott argued after Becka brought it up.

"Sure you did. Something like that."

"I never said I was a personal friend of the band. Darryl asked me how I got the tickets, and I said 'a close personal friend.' *He* said, 'You're friends with the band?' I just didn't say otherwise."

"You nodded as you closed the door," Becka argued. "And you *know* Darryl is out telling everyone that you're pals with The Scream."

Scott's face lit up. "You think so? Cool."

"It's not exactly telling the truth, Scotty. I can't believe you'd lie to your best friend like that. That's not cool with God."

Scott looked defensive. "It's not exactly lying, Becka."

"Mom might have other ideas . . . and I know Dad would." Bringing up God and their deceased father didn't seem fair. Becka regretted what she said as soon as she saw the look on Scott's face. She touched his arm. "Forget it. I don't care what your friends think anyway."

Scott nodded. That obviously was fine with him.

Becka changed the subject. "I think we

should at least e-mail Z. We should find out why it's so important to him that we see The Scream."

"Why?" Scott asked as Mom entered the room with laundry.

"We need more information," Becka answered. "Right now all we know is that we're supposed to meet their drummer."

"All you knew in Transylvania was that you were supposed to meet Jaimie Baylor," Scott replied. "The rest just happens . . . kinda like falling off a log."

"I hope those phony vampire attacks in Transylvania are not your idea of falling off a log." Becka scowled as she headed into the kitchen.

A moment later Mom followed her. "What's the matter, honey?" Mom asked. "You don't want to go to L.A.?"

"It's not really that," Becka answered. "It's just . . . The Scream . . . I mean, they're popular and all, but they're really into the black-magic stuff—skulls, pentagrams, and stuff like that. I know most of it's just an act . . . but it's not an act I really want to see."

Mom nodded. "That's not the kind of group I'd want you listening to, much less associating with."

"Me either," Becka agreed.

"But . . ."

"But what?"

"Maybe Z figures that by sending us, we'll help them somehow."

Becka knew Mom was right. That's how it had always been with Z. He always sent them someplace to help out in some way. And Becka knew something else, too. She knew her reluctance to go wasn't about whether or not she liked the music. It was about whether or not she wanted to help the people making that music.

And the truth was, part of her didn't. As far as she could tell, they were too into satanic stuff. Maybe they were nice guys under all that goop and three-foot hair. But they were definitely not her idea of good company.

And yet, if they needed help . . .

"I guess we should probably pray about it," Becka said with a sigh.

Mom smiled. "I'm proud of you for suggesting that. One of the reasons Z selected you is because you're cautious. But when it comes to making decisions, you always let God have his way."

~

Mike Parsek sat in the back of the limo as it came to a halt. It was one of three stretch limos that pulled up in front of the Regent Beverly Wilshire Hotel. Mike was in no hurry to get out as he watched The Scream's entourage pour out of the cars. The other three members of the band got out of the first limo. Out of the second came two publicists, one road manager, a sound engineer, a light guy, and four roadies. Mike shared the third limo with clothes and guitars.

He was the last to enter the hotel lobby, where the scene was taking on epic proportions. It never ceased to amaze him. Wherever the band went, they were like modern-day kings. Wherever one of the band members turned, there was someone to wait on him. Then, of course, there were the fans—screaming and begging for autographs.

Mike and the others signed a few autographs and exchanged small talk with a segment of their adoring legion. Then Doland nodded slightly to the three burly security men waiting nearby. Instantly the hulks moved into action and smoothly separated the crowd from the band.

The security guys were pros. Their sheer massiveness eased the crowd away as they escorted the band to the elevator. Mike gave a sigh of relief. By now the road manager had secured their rooms, and the publicists and tech guys scrambled for what accommodations were left. The roadies would go on to the auditorium and set up for most of the night. Then they'd sleep in the van.

Twenty minutes later, Mike and the other

band members were in one of their rooms eating steak sandwiches and drinking exotic-looking bottles of beer made in the African country of Chad. It was bottled especially for them by a guy in Trenton, New Jersey, whom they paid a thousand dollars a week for the service. Actually, *they* didn't pay it. Their record label did—just like it paid for a hundred other little extras that came under the heading of "touring expenses." Mike couldn't help but smile. Yessir, the rock music industry wasn't a conservative business.

"I think we should start with 'Army of the Night' tomorrow," Tommy Doland said between sips of beer. "It's what they want to hear."

Jackie Vee polished his guitar. It was a 1956 Gibson Les Paul—worth thousands of dollars. It seldom left his side. "We can if you want." He shrugged. "Only don't we usually save it for a grand finale at the end of the night?"

Doland swigged his beer. "I just want to get it over with. Get all the blasted shouting over with up front so we can enjoy the rest of the gig."

Mike knew that it was best for him to stay out of Doland's way during such discussions, but he couldn't resist. "You don't want them to cheer?"

"Of course I want them to cheer!" Doland

snapped. "I want them to pass out from screaming their heads off. But I don't want them calling out for 'Army of the Night' all night long and not paying attention to our other songs—especially the new ones, the ones *not* on the CD."

Mike nodded. "But that new stuff hasn't been going over with the audience like some of our older—"

"That's 'cause they don't listen!" Doland interrupted. There was no missing the edge to his voice. "We've got to help them get into these new songs."

"Some say the new songs are way too dark," Mike said so softly that he almost wasn't heard.

But Doland heard. "They're too dark because the idiots don't understand what we're trying to say!" he growled, then paused as a smile crossed his face again. "Like some of you," he went on, his mocking eyes riveted on Mike, "they just don't *get* it." With that, he patted Mike on the head, then headed to his room.

Mike watched him go, then turned to watch Grant Simone while he sanded the frets on his bass guitar with a worn piece of sandpaper. "See what I mean?" Mike said. "That's how he is all the time now."

Grant shrugged. "Whatever . . . Say, I'm thinking about redoing these frets again."

Mike shook his head. "If you'd stop sanding them all the time, they'd last longer. Listen, don't you guys think Doland is acting weird?"

"So what?" Jackie piped up. "So the pressure is getting to him a little. I didn't hear you asking to be left out of the limo, Mikey."

Grant nodded. "Or these fancy rooms or the fame or the chicks—"

"Or all that beautiful, cold, hard cash." Jackie grinned.

Mike looked at them both, wanting to respond, to tell them they were wrong . . . but he couldn't. They were right.

He looked away and let out a sad, lonely sigh.

~

Becka still felt unsure about the trip, even on Sunday morning as she packed. The whole family had come to look forward to these "little getaways." The time spent traveling reminded Becka of their missionary days in South America.

But this time something bugged her about the trip. It was way down deep in her stomach. She couldn't seem to ignore it. Earlier, they'd all prayed and felt that the trip was something God wanted them to do. But still . . .

She had tried to contact Z earlier on the Internet, but he didn't respond. He hadn't sent them any messages either. For the time being at least, it looked like they were on their own.

"Hurry up, Becka! It's almost nine-thirty!" Mom called from the kitchen. It was nearly time to leave for church. Becka had been dawdling, thinking about what it would be like to be in L.A. with Mom, her goofy brother, and four guys who wore capes, painted symbols on their faces, and had hair longer than hers.

"Hey, Beck, where's my leather jacket?" Scott called from his room.

"You don't have a leather jacket!" Becka answered. "It's mine!"

"Well, where's *yours*, then?"

"In my closet, where it belongs . . . And no, you can't borrow it again!"

"Why not?"

Becka sighed. "Because last time you left it outside in the sun with a candy bar in the pocket, remember?"

"Oh yeah. C'mon, Beck! I promise I won't do that. It's too early for candy. Mom doesn't let me eat it in church anyway."

Sometimes Becka couldn't believe her brother. "That's not the point. I told you you couldn't wear it again if you didn't take care of it."

"I took care of it. I just forgot about the candy bar, that's all."

"You also left it wadded up on the floor."

"So?" Scott clearly did not have a clue what the problem was here.

"So, you were supposed to hang it up."

"I leave *all* my clothes on the floor."

"I'll vouch for that," Mom said, joining in. "You guys better hurry and get dressed. We have to go if we're going to make church and still catch that plane."

Scott tapped on Becka's door. "Beck . . . c'mon. I need that jacket."

Becka combed her hair in front of the dresser mirror. "No."

Scott was persistent. "Can I come in?"

With another sigh, she opened the door. "Why? You can't borrow my jacket. And *where* did you get that shirt? Mom's not going to let you wear that to church."

It was the official Scream T-shirt. Four hairy guys scowling and holding skulls in their hands. "It's Darryl's," Scott answered. "And I'm not wearing it to church. Just let me borrow the jacket. You can borrow something of mine."

Becka closed her eyes for a moment. It just wasn't worth the fight. With a shake of her head, she opened up her closet and pulled out the jacket. "Here. I'm surprised you can still fit in it since you're taller than me now." At seventeen, Becka was about five feet six. "Just be nice to me on the plane."

"I always am," Scott said, grabbing the

jacket from her. "I can do anything for an hour and twenty-minute trip! . . . Thanks, Beck! This trip is gonna be awesome!"

Once again Becka felt a woozy sensation deep in her stomach.

∾

Half an hour later, Becka felt calmer, now that they were in church. The service helped a little. The worship team led the singing of one of Becka's favorite songs, and the drama team put on a funny skit. Finally, she felt herself relax . . . until the pastor began his sermon.

"I want to ask you this morning, why do you suppose that Jesus dined with tax collectors and prostitutes?" he began. "Do you think there was better food in that part of town?"

Several people chuckled as the pastor continued, "Do you think he enjoyed the company of those individuals more than he did the company of priests and scribes? Well, maybe he did, even though many people despised tax collectors, because they collected taxes for Rome. We know that Jesus was not a big fan of hypocrisy. The Pharisees were loaded with it! But I think the real reason why Jesus dined with what was considered a bunch of lowlifes was that he wanted to reach them. He wanted to share the good news of God's kingdom with them. He didn't come just for the priests and scribes. He came for *all* people. How could he expect these people to accept what he was saying if he didn't accept them? They were sinners, to be sure. But aren't we all? Fortunately, Jesus sees beyond that. He sees all of us—social outcasts or not—as people he dearly loves."

Becka's stomach churned like a cement mixer, but her mind remained focused on the pastor's words. She knew that she had heard from God.

"Yes," the pastor continued, "Jesus is also the great Judge. But he didn't come to judge—not then. He came to love those who were trapped in darkness. And love begins with acceptance . . . not of the sin, but of the sinner. As those who seek to follow Christ, can we do any less? We're called not only to accept those who are different from us but also to go the extra mile to bond with them, just as the apostle Paul did on his missionary journeys. We need to understand those who are lost so we can speak to their hearts. That doesn't mean that we agree with all of the choices the people we reach have made. It just means that we're willing to share God's love with them. Jesus reached out to prostitutes and tax collectors. Who are the lost *we* are to reach?"

Becka slowly nodded. *OK, Lord, I get it.*
And she did. She was going to L.A. She was
going to meet the band. She would talk with
them, hang out with them . . . even accept
them. And when the time came, she would
have the courage to speak God's truth to
them.

At least, she hoped she would.

3

The main airport in Los Angeles was LAX. That's what the people called it. No long fancy name after some former city politician. No warm-fuzzy sounding name with *hills* or *briar* or *crest* in it. Just the basic deal.

It was very L.A.

From the plane, Becka and Scott could see mountains, but they'd seen mountains before—bigger ones than these—back in South America. They could also see the ocean, but they'd seen that before, too. It really wasn't until they were on the ground in the airport that they began to see the real sights of L.A.

"Hey, isn't that Suzanne Winters?" Scott piped up as soon as they reached the baggage-claim area. "You know—the TV star. Right over there."

"Scott, don't point," Becka whispered in embarrassment. "People don't like that."

"How would you know?" he retorted. "How many stars have *you* seen?"

"C'mon, kids! Let's get our bags!" Mom called.

Out in the parking lot, they caught a shuttle to their hotel. "Why do they call it a shuttle?" Scott wanted to know. "It's a bus."

"They call it a shuttle because it goes back and forth between the hotel and the airport," Becka explained.

"Yeah, I know," Scott replied. "A bus."

Becka blew her thin, brown hair out of her eyes and heaved her suitcase up into the luggage area. As they headed up the freeway on-ramp, they could see heavy smoke off in the distance.

"What's that?" Becka asked. "Looks like a big fire."

A man sitting across from them said,

"There's a brush fire burning out of control in the mountains. It's headed toward Malibu."

"Wow!" Scott replied, in awe of the great pillars of smoke.

Becka's stomach churned. She winced slightly and shifted in her seat.

Mom turned to her. "What's the matter, honey?"

"Oh, it's just my stomach. That sure looks like a huge fire."

"No biggie," Scott said, suddenly sounding very authoritative. "There's some kind of natural disaster going on almost every day in Los Angeles. My geography teacher said the place is like a natural-disaster theme park."

Somehow that didn't help Becka's stomach.

Eventually the shuttle cruised into Beverly Hills.

"Cool!" Scott exclaimed, his face glued to the window. "This is where a lot of the movie stars live. Check out the size of that house." He pointed to a home roughly the size of a museum.

"And look at those shops," Becka added, pointing in a different direction. "Could we do some shopping while we're here, Mom?"

Mom nodded. "A little. But not at those places, honey. That's Rodeo Drive."

She pronounced it *Ro-day-o* Drive, but Scott hadn't heard. He also read the sign.

"It says Rodeo Drive," he mused. "You don't want to shop there, Beck. Probably all cowboy clothes and stuff like that."

"Scotty," Becka snickered, "people all over the world know that stores on Rodeo Drive have the coolest clothes. I thought even *you* would know that."

"And they're *very* expensive," Mom added.

"That's *so* L.A.," Scott quipped. "They expect you to pay a fortune for cowboy clothes."

Before Becka could respond, the shuttle pulled into the hotel parking lot. Just as it did, her breath caught. She quickly exchanged glances with Scott and Mom. The place was huge, as well as beautiful. Bellhops were everywhere, loading baggage onto little golden carts. Rich people in expensive clothes strolled back and forth. And just outside Scott's window was the longest car he'd ever seen.

"Look at that!" he exclaimed. "It's like a double limo!"

"They call that a stretch," the man across the aisle said.

"No wonder," Scott replied. "Must be a stretch to afford it."

They watched as a man with expensive-looking sunglasses and hair a mixture of coal black and bright blue climbed out of the stretch limo and walked toward the hotel.

But just before he headed up the steps, he stopped suddenly, then slowly turned and stared at the shuttle bus.

"Hey, isn't that Tommy Doland?" Scott asked as they headed for the door of the bus. Becka nodded. "Why do you suppose he's looking at us?" she asked, feeling her stomach tighten again.

No one had an answer.

Doland stood there, watching the people get off the shuttle. Becka was the first to reach the exit. As she stepped down the stairs, she glanced up to see the singer still staring. He had taken off his dark sunglasses and looked like he was trying to glare a hole right through her.

She felt a cold shiver run through her body. She clutched her throat, unable to breathe suddenly.

Tommy Doland suddenly snapped his sunglasses back on and hurried up the steps to the hotel.

It took a moment for Becka to start breathing again.

"He was looking right at you!" Scott exclaimed in excitement.

She nodded, feeling numb.

"You should have said something! At least waved. I bet he could have taken us right to Mike Parsek."

"Those are not our instructions," Becka

said, finally finding her voice. "We're supposed to see him after the show. Besides . . ."

"Besides what?" Scott pressed as they
headed toward the hotel.

Becka looked at her brother and frowned.
She had felt the same sensation she had
experienced a couple of months ago when
battling some evil spirits that had taken up
residence in her best friend, Julie.

Becka swallowed and finally answered,
"When he was staring at me, it was like I
couldn't speak. Like I was choking—" She
met her brother's eyes. "Scotty, I couldn't
breathe."

~

Mike detected the faint smell of marijuana
smoke the moment he knocked on Jackie
Vee's hotel-room door. There was no answer,
so he knocked again. Then the door opened
slowly, and Jackie peered out at him.

"Hey, Jackie. Got a minute?"

"Sure. C'mon in."

As soon as Mike closed the door, Jackie
took out a small silver case, about the size of
a pack of cigarettes. He opened it and took
out a joint. From the looks of him, it wasn't
his first. "Want to get high, man?"

Mike shook his head. "No. It throws off my
timing. We've got to rehearse in a couple of
hours. . . . I hope tonight's show goes well. I

want us to feel really good for that cable broadcast. Forty million viewers, man."

Jackie nodded. "Should be good. Will Billy be back for that?"

"Should be. I talked to him a while ago. He's outta the hospital. Sounds like he's doing pretty well. You should call him."

Jackie took a long hit off the joint and stared blankly into space.

"I said you should call him," Mike repeated.

Jackie looked up, squinting like he was trying to focus. "What? . . . Oh yeah." He waved his hand dismissively. "I'm too tired to call him now. Maybe after rehearsal."

Mike nodded, but he knew Jackie would never remember to call. He probably wouldn't even remember this conversation. "Listen," he asked, "what are we going to do about Doland? I can hardly talk to him anymore."

"He's off on his own trip, that's for sure," Jackie agreed. "But he gets the crowd going, doesn't he? He plays the audience like I play this guitar."

Mike pressed the issue. "I talked to him about Billy getting hurt. It was like he didn't even care. He just said it would sell more CDs."

Jackie took another hit. "Probably will. Doland knows that stuff."

"Yeah," Mike agreed. "But does he care about anybody?"

Jackie didn't seem to hear. He took another hit, staring at nothing. Mike knew from past experience that the conversation was over. Jackie was too high to listen to anything that required thought. He stood up. "I've gotta go. See you at rehearsal."

He was halfway down the hall before he heard Jackie call after him, "OK . . . See ya, Mike."

He headed for the elevator and pushed the button. A moment later, the door opened to reveal Tommy Doland.

"Doland . . . I . . ." Doland's sudden appearance startled him. Mike felt guilty, like he'd been "caught" being disloyal.

Doland smiled, but there was something very unpleasant in the way his lips curled. "Hi ya, Mikey. Is your room on this floor? No, that's right. Your room is on the sixth floor. Jackie's room is here . . . just down the hall, right?"

"Right." Mike tried to smile. "We were just—" He broke off. Doland's smile had turned to ice.

"I know what you were doing, Mikey. You were trying to turn Jackie against me."

Mike stared at him, stunned—and very uneasy at the look in Doland's eyes. "No, I wasn't . . . not really. I'm just worried."

"You should be worried, Mikey. You cross me again and I'll fry you."

Mike was shocked by the threat. "What? *Fry* me? What is *that* supposed to—?"

Doland cut him off. "Fry you? My, my, getting a bit paranoid, aren't we?" He smiled again, his eyes glazing over. "I said I'd *fire* you, Mikey . . . from the band." The smile broadened. "You just need to be more careful now, don't you? When you listen to people, I mean." Doland stood there in the elevator, glaring at Mike as the steel door closed, leaving Mike staring blankly at it.

~

"This place is unbelievable," Scott muttered as he studied his reflection in the mirrored walls of the elevator. "It's so cool that Z booked us a suite in this huge place!"

Becka shook her head. It didn't take much to entertain some people.

Just then there was a loud ding. As the elevator door opened, she moved to step out. "Our floor, Scott—" She broke off suddenly and stared in surprise. There, right in front of her, was Mike Parsek. In fact, if she hadn't known better, Becka could have sworn he'd been staring at the elevator, waiting for them.

Scott recognized him immediately. "Uh . . ." But for the first time in his life he seemed speechless.

Becka grabbed his arm and pulled him from the elevator as Mike moved past them to enter it. At last Scott found his voice . . . well, at least some of it. "Hey, hi . . . uh . . ."

But as Mike turned and the elevator doors closed, he was not looking at Scott. His gaze was locked on Becka. And he seemed very impressed.

The two stood in stunned silence. Finally, Scott spoke. "Wow! Did you see him check you out?"

Becka was dumbfounded. Most of the boys back at school didn't even know she existed. But clearly this guy did. And he just happened to be a rock star!

"That was Mike Parsek!" Scott exclaimed. "He's the one we're supposed to talk to! Why didn't you say something?"

Becka tried to swallow, but her mouth was as dry as cotton. "Why didn't you?" she finally croaked.

"I did!" Scott insisted. "I asked him how he was."

"Oh, really? 'Cause all I heard was, 'Hey, hi . . . uh.'"

Scott turned red. "Yeah, well, at least I said something. You were afraid to even talk to him."

Becka took a deep breath and nodded. "You're right. I was." She slowly turned to her little brother, feeling very uneasy and very concerned. "And maybe . . . maybe you should be, too."

~

That evening Becka and Mom got ready for the concert while Scott played with his laptop computer.

"You'd better hurry and get ready, Scotty," Mom called from one of the rooms of the suite. "We're leaving in fifteen minutes."

"I *am* ready," he replied, keeping his voice calm. "Hey, Beck, I'm checking out The Scream's Web site. You should see it. The whole thing comes out of this huge skull."

"Why am I not surprised?"

"What do you mean you're ready?" Mom yelped as she stepped into the room and stared at Scott's attire: a worn, torn sweatshirt, dirty jeans, and beat-up joggers.

"This is what you're *supposed* to wear to the concert," Scott explained in his most patient voice. "This is what *everyone* will be wearing—everyone but you and Becka."

"Really?" Mom asked in surprise. "But you . . . you look . . . so . . . destitute."

"'Destitute at the Institute.'"

"What?"

"That's a Scream song. You know, 'Destitute at the Institute, but alive in my mind.'"

Mom grimaced. "This is going to be a difficult evening for me, isn't it?"

Scott nodded. "Yes, Mom. I imagine it will be."

She sighed slowly. "All right. You can wear everything but the sweatshirt."

"Mom!" Scott protested.

"It stinks."

"But . . . it's the coolest thing I've got."

"Well, I want you to take it off."

Becka joined the conversation. "Mom, the sweatshirt is the focus of his entire outfit. It goes with his jogging shoes, right, Scott?"

He tossed her a grateful look. "Yeah . . . exactly . . . what she said."

Mom nodded. "I see. And I still say it stinks—literally. It smells, because you haven't washed it in a month. So . . . change it."

"All right," Scott finally conceded, mostly because he was more interested in what was happening on his computer than in continuing the conversation. "I've got a message coming in."

In the lower left-hand corner of the screen was a blinking yellow *Z*, signaling that a message was coming through. Scott had created the little *Z* symbol and programmed his computer so that the symbol would pop up whenever an e-mail message arrived. He would have liked to make the symbol come on only when the message was from Z, but Z's address always changed. That was part of the mystery of Z—the person they had never met, but who always seemed to know what was going on in their lives.

"Hey, it's Z!" Scott called after the message appeared. "Check it out."

Becka joined him. Together the two read silently:

> Greetings. Hope you enjoy the hotel.
> I have two pieces of information.
> 1. Your mission is Mike Parsek. He is
> a pastor's son, but has not communicated
> with his father for several years. He knows
> the truth from his childhood, but he's
> in over his head. He has no concept of the
> danger he's in.
> 2. Beware of Tommy Doland.

Becka felt a chill as she read the warning. Her eyes dropped to the bottom of the screen, where Z had written a brief Scripture. It wasn't long, but it was enough to remind her of the seriousness of their task:

> "Be careful! Watch out for attacks from the
> Devil, your great enemy. He prowls around like
> a roaring lion, looking for some victim to devour.
> Take a firm stand against him, and be strong
> in your faith" (1 Peter 5:8-9).

Scott didn't seem to even see the warning or the verse. Instead, he pointed his finger to the number *1* on the screen. "See?" He smiled smugly. "I told you you should've talked to Parsek."

Becka shrugged. "What makes Z think these people will listen to us anyway?"

"Not 'these people,'" Scott corrected. "Mike Parsek. And I'd say by the way he scoped you out earlier that he'd be willing to listen to anything you say."

Becka's face flamed. She turned quickly, grabbed her coat, and headed for the door. Scott snapped off the computer and followed, smiling. Being a pesky little brother definitely had its advantages at times.

～

The Forum in Los Angeles held about twenty thousand people, and it was jam-packed. But Becka wasn't bothered by the size of the crowd. Instead, she worried about the attitude of the crowd.

Everyone in the place seemed angry— maybe even beyond angry. Most of them seemed ready to explode. Small groups huddled together, scowling at the groups surrounding them. It was the most explosive group of people Becka had ever seen under one roof.

And there are twenty thousand of them. All here.

She glanced at Mom. From the expression on her face, things seemed equally bizarre to Mom. Her mouth gaped open. Becka knew that Scott's comment about torn sweatshirts and faded jeans had been an understatement. Becka hadn't had the heart to tell Mom that.

One guy had three safety pins in his left eyebrow. Another had a stud through his nose and one through his lip. And one girl, clad all in leather, had four Scream buttons pinned to her lower lip.

This was definitely not Mom's kind of place.

"I had no idea that it'd be this . . . this . . . bad!" she shouted as they made their way toward their seats. "Maybe I should have stayed at the hotel."

"You can go back if you want, Mom!" Scott shouted. "We can catch a cab back ourselves."

Mom's response was immediate. "Forget that thought, young man," she said firmly. "Now that I've seen what this concert is like, I'm glad I came here with you." She shook her head. "I'll be glad when this thing is over."

As they took their seats, Becka felt the tension in the air increase. The band was late getting started, which made the crowd even rowdier.

But suddenly—

WHAM! WHAM! BOOOOOOOOM!

The sound of explosions came from the

stage. The crowd roared. As the curtain rose, the spotlights came on, bathing a huge skull in reds, blues, and yellows. Doland's voice could be heard.

Army of the night,
Not afraid to fight!

Doland suddenly appeared in the spotlight. He screamed into the microphone as the guitar wailed and the bass and drums pounded the beat. Everyone in the crowd leaped to their feet, screaming.

Everyone but Becka. She couldn't explain it, but she suddenly felt nauseous.

"Becky, what's the matter?!" Mom shouted. She also remained in her seat.

"Nothing!" she replied. "It's just my stomach again! I'll be OK!"

"Maybe it was something you ate!"

Becka nodded, but she knew that wasn't the reason for her stomach trouble. She'd felt this before. She always felt this way when she encountered something demonic. And looking up at the stage, at Doland's blazing eyes as he shrieked the song, Becka knew with sudden certainty that the skulls and other symbols of satanism were far more than props.

There was something very real—and very frightening—going on here.

4

The intensity of the crowd built and subsided in perfect rhythm with the music and pacing of the show. As the band neared the end of their performance, there was one climax after another, with each new one topping the last. By the time Mike launched into his drum solo, the mood of the crowd had been driven to a feverish pitch.

More and more effects were released. Two large fog machines at each end of the stage shot out a mist that quickly enshrouded the bottom three feet of the stage. But Becka's eyes were drawn away from the fog to the huge dragon cannon. So far it had remained a silent yet ominous presence. With firepots and other effects cutting loose all night from unseen places, one couldn't help but wonder what this big machine might do when fired. From her seat in the third row, Becka could see the top of the cannon rising just above the fog.

It began to vibrate.

She felt the urge to pray. *That's silly*, she thought to herself. *I'm not wasting energy worrying about some special effect. It's what the band wants—to freak people out and make them think there's real danger when everything is under control.*

Still, the dragon cannon bothered her. And the harder Mike played, the more it vibrated, as if preparing to fire.

Becka glanced at Scott. He appeared to be watching Doland, plainly enthralled with the show.

Several times during the evening, Becka had exchanged glances with Scott. He also seemed to feel that something strange was going on. She felt good about his silent agreement. But she knew that Scott wouldn't let a weird feeling spoil his good time.

"Scotty—" Becka nudged him—"let me see your binoculars for a minute." She had been about to criticize him for bringing them, since they were in the third row. But now she was glad that he brought them.

She knew he didn't appreciate the interruption, but he handed them to her anyway. She focused on the dragon cannon. It was definitely vibrating. Again she felt the urge to pray but dismissed it as a childish fear.

Then she saw something that made her blood run cold.

One of the large bolts holding the cannon in place had come loose. With every vibration of the cannon, the bolt slipped more and more out of place. Any second now it would fall out completely!

Becka wasn't sure what that meant. She directed the binoculars to the opposite side of the cannon. The other bolt seemed solidly in place. Her stomach knotted as she wondered whether or not she should do something or tell somebody.

The tempo of Mike's drumming increased. Scott reached for his binoculars, but Becka shrugged him off. She stared at the bolt as it shook back and forth. Suddenly, it fell out, disappearing into the fog.

Now, with only one bolt holding the cannon, the great machine shifted slightly with each vibration. The icy fear gripping Becka grew as she watched the cannon turn. *Oh, Jesus,* she prayed, no longer dismissing the urging as childish. *Jesus, protect them!* No one onstage appeared to notice, yet the cannon slowly turned in an entirely different direction.

She felt Scott tapping her on the shoulder, but she wasn't about to give the binoculars back. As the drum solo reached a crescendo, the cannon vibrated even more.

It was about to fire!

And the more it vibrated, the more it turned, until it was pointing directly at the band. More specifically, it was aimed at Mike Parsek!

God, don't let this happen! Don't let it end like this before we even get a chance to talk with him! Becka's lips moved as she prayed. Through the binoculars she saw a roadie crossing behind the band to some kind of control panel. A spark of hope surged through her.

Please, God, help him see that the cannon is loose.

But the roadie didn't notice. Instead, he flipped some switches on the control panel. The cannon shook even harder, but it could turn no farther.

It was about to fire!

Becka watched the roadie press another button. A deep rumble began, even louder than Mike's drums. The cannon's firing mechanism ignited. She couldn't bear to look, but she couldn't bear to look away.

Mike reached the peak of his solo. He glanced to the side and suddenly saw the barrel pointing directly at him. But it was too late. The cannon ignited. . . .

But it did not fire.

Something had malfunctioned. Becka saw Mike shouting at the stagehand, frantically motioning for him to shut down the device. The stagehand leaped into action, and the cannon stopped vibrating.

Everyone was safe.

Becka knew why the cannon had failed to fire. Her prayer had been answered! Not exactly in the way she had prayed, but answered nonetheless. And for that she offered up another prayer—this time, a prayer of thanks.

~

Before the final note of the show was finished, Scott was already on his feet. He knew what they had to do. "Let's hurry up and get backstage!"

"They just got done, Scotty!" Becka shouted, her ears still ringing from the loud music. "Shouldn't we give them a few minutes?"

"Are you kidding?! In a few minutes there will be a hundred people in front of us trying to squeeze their way in!" He glanced toward the door closest to the stage. Already, scores of kids lined up, hoping for a glimpse of one of the band members.

"But we have passes!" Mom reminded him. She, too, talked loudly, as if trying to talk over the concert noises.

Scott nodded, trying to get them moving even as he talked. "I know, Mom! But you've got to show your pass to the guy at the door before he'll let you through! And before you can show your pass, you've got to get to the guy! And that'll be harder with every second we wait! Come on!!"

"He's right!" Becka nodded. "We'd better go!"

The three of them made their way to the stage door. As they got close, Scott leaned over to Becka and whispered, "What about Mom?"

"What about her?"

"Maybe she shouldn't go back there with us. I mean, she doesn't fit in and . . ."

Becka looked at him blankly. It was obvious she wasn't going to help. "And what?"

"Well . . . you know." Scott fidgeted. "What are we going to say? 'Hi, Mike, we're Scott and Becka, and this is our mom'? Nobody brings their mom backstage."

Becka shrugged. "I don't think that's our decision, Scott."

"What do you mean?"

"Z is the one who sent the tickets and the passes. He must've wanted her to come along."

"What are you kids talking about?" Mom asked. Finally, her voice had returned to its normal volume. "If it's what I think it is, you needn't bother to discuss it."

For an instant Scott thought Mom was going to be a sport and let them go by themselves. But then she added, "I'm *going* with you. Who knows what might be going on back there?"

Scott sighed. Great. Here he was getting to do practically the coolest thing in the world and his mom had to tag along. He felt like a ten-year-old.

It took a while to get through the horde of kids pressing toward the door—but not as long as Scott had expected. There was one very simple reason for that:

Mom.

"Excuse me, sir!" she called out above the crowd to the burly guard at the stage door. "We have backstage passes! Would you let us through, please?"

Scott knew that would never have worked if he or Becka had shouted it. Either the guard would have thought they were lying or everyone in the crowd would have pounced on them and tried to take the passes.

But with a mother in the lead, it was totally different. Scott watched in amazement as the sea of rough-looking, pierced, and tattooed fans parted to let them through.

The big guy at the door eyed them suspiciously—that was his job—but as soon as he saw the passes, he immediately opened the door for them.

As they stepped inside, they noticed a party going full blast. All kinds of strange and interesting people stood around talking and laughing. None of the band members were around, however.

Scott turned to a tall guy with long blond dreadlocks. "Hey, excuse me. Could you tell me—?" he began, but the guy walked away without giving Scott a glance. Undaunted, Scott turned to a girl who had a fake ruby in her belly button and wore huge bell-bottoms. "Miss, uh . . . could you tell me where to find the band? We're supposed to meet them and—"

But the girl was already laughing. "Don't expect them for a while. It's way uncool for them to show up at their own party any earlier."

With that, she moved off toward a table of refreshments next to a huge bar. Scott shrugged and followed.

In the center of the table was a guitar made of salmon. The strings had been made with cream cheese and the tuning pegs were black olives on toothpicks. It must've been pretty good because several people scooped up crackers full of the stuff and wolfed them down. So, of course, Scott followed suit.

"Yuuuck!" he said loud enough to draw several disapproving looks. "This stuff tastes terrible!"

Now, even that wouldn't have been so bad, but there were a couple of minor additions. . . .

The first was when Scott tried to spit out the offending bite of salmon. The second was when he tried to get rid of the taste by eating some salsa. The *green* salsa. The *extra-hot* salsa.

He ran to the bar, hand over mouth, gesturing to the bartender for something to drink. The man started to hand him a beer but caught Mom's disapproving look and changed it to a bottled water. It didn't matter to Scott . . . as long as it was cool and wet. *Anything* to put out the fire.

After gulping down the water, Scott suddenly noticed at least a dozen people staring at him. He turned to Becka and whispered, "What are they looking at? We're at a backstage party, for cryin' out loud. Everything should be cool here. I mean, *look* at these people! Are you telling me you still have to do things a certain way or people stare?"

Becka sighed. "I think it's called having manners."

Before Scott could fire off a smart come-back, the room broke into applause. He turned to see the band's arrival at the party.

They had on different clothes than the ones they had worn on stage. Some of the band members' outfits were just as outra-geous as their stage clothes.

Doland headed straight for the bar, where he ordered a double shot of whiskey, gulped it down, then ordered a beer.

Scott gawked. Tommy Doland, the lead singer of The Scream, was less than five feet away from him! Amazing! And, to top it off, Doland turned and actually looked at him!

He sees me! Scott thought. *He's going to speak to me. We're gonna become friends!*

Doland stared at him a long moment before finally speaking. "Get lost, freak!"

Scott's mouth dropped open even farther. Everyone stared at him as if he had just thrown up in the punch bowl. It was a good thing there wasn't a punch bowl there, or he might have done just that.

And then, to make matters even worse, he saw Mom making a beeline for Doland. *Oh no!* he thought. *She's coming over to defend me!*

Fortunately, Mike intervened by walking up to Scott. "Are you Scott Williams? I'm Mike Parsek."

Scott tried to answer. He knew his mouth moved, but no sound came out of it.

Mike continued, "Z is a friend of mine on the Internet. He told me you'd be coming. How'd you like the show?"

"Uhhh . . . I . . . uh . . . good. . . . It was good." Scott knew that he sounded like an idiot. He threw a glance at Doland. Fortunately, the guy had already forgotten him and was nuzzling up to a girl wearing an extra-large Scream T-shirt and platforms so high she could hardly walk in them.

Scott turned back to Mike. By that point, the drummer had turned to Becka.

"You must be Rebecca," he said. He sounded a shade friendlier than he had with Scott. "How'd you like the show?"

Caught totally off guard, Becka did a repeat of her brother's stellar performance. "Uhhh . . . I . . . uh . . . good. It was good."

Mike laughed. "I can see a strong resemblance between you two. And this must be your mother," he continued. "Hello, Mrs. Williams. How are you?"

Mom smiled warmly and shook Mike's hand. "Very well, thank you. I'm not used to that sort of show, but I found it . . . fascinating."

"Thank you," Mike replied with a smile.

"Who're your friends, Mike?" It was Doland, his arm draped over the girl in the

T-shirt. He looked at Scott and smiled. Or was it a sneer?

"Lemme guess—they're from your daddy's church? Or maybe your Sunday school class?"

"Bug off, Doland," Mike replied. He turned back to Becka. "Nice to see you," was all he said before turning and walking away.

Doland snickered and also headed off.

Scott turned to Becka, looking disappointed. "That's it?"

"I guess so," Becka said, sounding as disappointed as he seemed to feel.

Scott shook his head. "So much for the world of heavy metal." How was he going to tell the guys back home about this? What a bust! "I guess we should go."

Becka agreed. "I guess we've done enough damage here for one night."

~

"Do you think going to that concert was a bad idea?" Becka asked Mom. Scott had gone for a late-night swim in the hotel pool, leaving Becka and Mom alone.

"No, honey," Mom answered. "The music was pretty loud though. I thought my ears would never stop ringing!"

"Some of the kids there kinda freaked me out a little," Becka continued. "Most of them seemed really angry. Even the band members seemed angry."

"Some of them were nice."

"*One* of them was," Becka corrected pointedly. "Part of me wants to get away from this place as fast as I can, but another part is saying that I should stop judging The Scream and try to help them. I must be crazy. I mean, these guys have the biggest-selling CD in the country, and I'm supposed to think they actually need *my* help?"

Mom smiled. "Maybe they do. Money doesn't give you peace. It certainly doesn't get you to heaven." She paused, then said, "That drummer, Mike, came from a decent home. I could tell that just talking to him. But he's mixed up with some pretty rough people. I can see why Z thinks he might get hurt."

"So, what am I supposed to do?" Becka sighed. "Run away from the bad stuff . . . or stick around and try to help fix it?"

"I guess that depends on what the Lord is telling you."

"What do you mean?"

"The Bible says we are to flee from evil."

"That's right," Becka agreed.

"But it also says we are to help people, to bring light into the darkness. The trick is to know what God wants you to do and when to do it. If you find your light growing dim because you're getting caught up in what the world's doing, then you should flee. But if your light is shining brightly, then maybe you should stick around for a while and see if you can light up the place with the help of the Holy Spirit."

"And how am I supposed to know the difference?" Becka asked.

Mom took a deep breath and slowly let it out. "I guess that's between you and God, isn't it?"

Becka nodded. As usual, Mom was right.

Twenty minutes later Becka was out on the balcony, all alone, staring out at the twinkling lights around Los Angeles.

She prayed silently. *Dear Lord, things are really weird this time around. I mean, I know you want us to reach out to these guys. I know you love them as much as you love me. But . . . how do you do it, Lord? How do you wade through a mud hole to help someone without getting muddy yourself? I really need your wisdom, Lord. I need to know what you would have me do.*

Becka paused for a moment, then continued, *I guess, to be honest, Lord, I really need your heart, too. I mean, I'm really tempted to just avoid the guys in The Scream. So help me see them— really see them—with the love you have for them. Thank you, Jesus. Amen.*

She opened her eyes, suddenly aware
that she felt better, but not because she
had an answer. She was just as clueless as she
was before she started praying. But she felt
better all the same because she knew that the
answer would come at the right time. And
that was enough.

The Scream was back onstage before a
packed auditorium as Mike blazed through
his drum solo. Once again the great cannon
began to vibrate as it prepared to fire. Only
this time it was not disguised as a dragon.
This time it was much bigger and far more
ominous.

Becka sat in the audience cheering, when
suddenly her expression turned to horror.
A gnarled, twisted hand, more animal than
human, snaked out from behind the curtain
and moved the giant cannon until it was
again pointed at Mike.

But he didn't seem to notice it. He just
kept playing, getting closer and closer to
the climactic moment.

Becka screamed, but he didn't hear her.

No one heard her.

And then it happened. Mike went into his
final crashing pattern. Suddenly, flames shot
from the huge cannon, engulfing him. He
stood up, staggered, and fell to the stage. He

was on fire, writhing in agony, rolling this way and that, trying to extinguish the flames. But nothing worked. Finally, his eyes met Becka's. He reached out his burned hands. His charred lips muttered something. She couldn't hear the words, but she knew what he was saying all the same.

"Help . . . me. Help . . . Please, help . . ."

Becka sat bolt upright, her chest heaving and her face bathed in sweat. She grappled for the light switch and turned it on. She was in bed in the room she shared with her mom. Her mom still slept peacefully in the double bed next to hers.

Becka pressed a trembling hand to her clammy face, trying to slow her pulse rate. The dream had been intense. But at least she had her answer. She would stay. Mike needed her to stay.

It made no sense—not as far as she could see. But as long as there was a chance that she could help, she would remain.

5

When Becka opened her eyes the next morning, the first thing she saw was Scott sitting in a chair at the foot of her bed eating a bowl of cereal. And the first thing she heard was: "You know something, Sis, Frosted Flakes taste even better from room service than they do from the box."

Becka looked at him through sleep-swollen eyes. "You woke me up to tell me that?"

"Not just that," Scott said. "I also wanted to tell you about my plan."

Becka sighed. "This better be good."

"No, listen. I've got an idea."

"You always do."

"Let him talk, honey," Mom called out from the bathroom.

"OK," Becka mumbled, "so talk."

"All right, here's what we do. We check out of this fancy hotel and cash in the rest of the vouchers Z sent us for housing. Then we check into a cheaper hotel and spend the money at Disneyland."

Becka rolled her eyes. "That's your plan?"

"It's better than going home. Or staying in this fancy-schmancy place and not being able to do anything else."

"I think we should stay where Z wants us to stay," Mom said, coming into the room. "And I do have a little extra money. Maybe later we could spend a day at Disneyland."

But Scott wasn't satisfied. "A day? I bet we could score enough on those vouchers to be there the rest of the week. Besides, Z only wanted us to stay here because this is where the band was staying while they got ready for their big cable TV show. And now that we're not seeing the band anymore, what's the point? I mean, this place is expensive. And for what . . . those little chocolates they leave on your pillow after they make the bed?"

"What chocolates?" Becka and Mom asked in unison.

Scott turned sheepish. "The ones I ate yesterday . . . all three of them."

They were interrupted by a knock at the door.

"I'll get it!" Becka said, throwing on her robe. "It's probably the maid with more chocolates. I want to be sure I get some this time."

But it wasn't the maid. When she opened up the door, she found Mike Parsek standing there. And instead of chocolates, he held out a rose. "Hi," he said, smiling at a very shocked Becka. "This is for you."

Becka couldn't say a word. All she could think about was her morning hair . . . her morning face . . . her morning everything. She tried to smooth down her hair.

Fortunately, Mom came to the rescue. "Mike, how nice to see you. Why don't you come in for a while?" She nudged the dumb-founded Becka aside to let Mike enter the room. Becka flashed off into the bedroom to throw on some clothes. Any clothes would be an improvement over her robe and Crescent Bay T-shirt.

As she hurriedly dressed, all the while wishing that she had time to jump into the shower, she could hear her mom making small talk. "So, how did you find our room number?"

"Oh, Z gave it to me. I found it in my e-mail this morning."

"Cool," Scott chirped.

"Anyway, I just came by to see if Becka would maybe like to go out for lunch."

Becka had chosen that moment to make her entrance in her most flattering jeans and a top that matched her eyes. At first she was astonished by Mike's announcement, then flattered, and finally a little bugged. "I appreciate the invite, Mike, but . . ."

"But what?"

Becka shrugged. "I don't know. Could I ask you one question first?"

"Fire away."

"Why did you leave like that? Last night, I mean. As soon as Tommy Doland came over, you walked away without hardly saying a word."

"Ah." He nodded.

"And now you show up here with a rose and everything. I mean, I'm flattered, but . . . what's going on?"

"That's a good question," Mike answered, "but not an easy one. Let's just say that Tommy Doland is not someone you want to know."

"You acted like it was you who didn't want to know us," Becka said.

"I know. It's just that . . . well, sometimes he likes to make fun of my friends."

"That's pretty lame," Scott muttered from

across the room. He suddenly looked embarrassed that he had spoken aloud.

Mike looked at him, then nodded. "You're right, it is. But if you give me another chance by going to lunch with me, maybe I can explain it better."

"OK," Scott said. "I'm willing to give it a shot."

Becka turned and glared at him. "I think he means *me.*"

"Yeah." Mike grinned. "I meant Rebecca."

Scott snorted in disgust.

"Sorry, Scott." Mike shrugged. "But if you're going to be in town, we could sure use some extra help setting up for the cable gig. Nothing too heavy. Just odds and ends. But we'd pay you twenty-five bucks an hour."

"Twenty-five bucks an—" Scott caught his breath and then tried again. Becka smiled as he did his best to respond with some semblance of being cool. "OK, I'll consider it . . . but only if you'll sign some things for my friends that I brought from home."

"Sure. And if you don't mind, maybe I can throw in a signed copy of our latest CD for you."

"You'd do that for—?" Once again Scott's voice cracked, and once again he fought to sound cool. "Yeah, uh, I think that would be all right."

There was no missing the chuckles all around the group.

Becka turned to Mom. "So, is it OK if I go to lunch with Mike?"

"Will you be eating in the hotel?" Mom asked.

Mike shook his head. "The hotel is too . . . popular. There's a nice café just down the block. I can give you my cell-phone number if you want."

"All right." Mom nodded. "Just don't be gone too long."

Mike wrote down the number. "I'll be back to pick you up around 11:30, Rebecca."

As soon as he left, Becka raced into the shower, trying hard not to grin.

Later as Mike and Becka headed out the door, Mike turned back to Scott. "Listen, if you can be ready to work in a couple of hours, you can ride with me over to the auditorium. They're going to mike the drums for a sound check."

"Great," Scott replied. "But . . . what about Doland? He didn't seem to like me very much last night."

"Just act like you've never met him. He was too stoned to remember anything about last night. That's how he always gets."

～

One floor above, Doland's room looked as if it had been trashed the night before. Doland appeared to be passed out on the sofa, as if sleeping off the effects of partying. But Doland wasn't passed out. His eyelids fluttered wildly. Strange noises—more like grunts and growls than words—came out of his mouth. One word formed on his lips again and again. It was a name . . .

Rebecca.

〰

Becka could hardly believe that she was having lunch with Mike Parsek in a stylish Beverly Hills café. She wondered what her friends back in Crescent Bay would say if they knew.

Her eyes widened when she saw the menu. Three-fifty for a Coke?! Get real! But Mike didn't seem to notice. Apparently, he was used to this kind of place.

"So how do you like L.A.?" he asked her as they set the menus aside.

She shrugged. "It's OK, I guess. I really haven't seen much of it yet."

Mike smiled. "Well, if you've got the afternoon free, we can fix that. After the sound check, I'll give you a personal tour, all right?"

Becka caught her breath. She was still having trouble believing that Mike—a celebrity—was so interested in spending time with her. But somehow she forced herself to stay cool. "That'd be nice. 'Course I'll have to check with Mom first, but it sounds like a lot of fun." She almost wished she didn't have to check with her mom.

When the waiter arrived, Becka ordered the shrimp scampi, but Mike ordered a plain old cheeseburger. As soon as the waiter had gone, Becka asked, "Are you sure this place is all right? I mean, we could cancel our order and go somewhere else."

Mike looked surprised. "I thought you liked this place."

"Oh, I do. I just wondered if it might be too expensive."

Mike laughed. It was a nice, easy laugh. Even though she knew he was laughing at what she said, she didn't feel embarrassed. "Don't worry about the price," he said. "I told you I'd take you out to lunch."

"B-but . . . ," Becka stammered.

"But what?"

"But you only ordered a cheeseburger."

Mike grinned. "What's wrong with that?"

"Nothing. I just thought that maybe you ordered one to save money. . . . I mean, with all the fancy things on the menu here." She suddenly realized how foolish she sounded. Mike Parsek's band was the hottest in the country. Of course he could afford lunch!

Mike laughed again. "I like cheeseburgers. More than all that fancy stuff. I mean, the other stuff is OK and everything, but once you've tried all the different kinds of food . . . well, cheeseburgers still taste the best."

"Oh, good . . ." Becka let out a sigh. "I'm glad." She paused for a moment and then continued, "You know, you really seem different from the other guys in the band." She couldn't help noticing the sadness in his eyes, even though he continued to smile. "I mean, the other guys seem so serious . . . kind of glum or mad . . . especially Tommy Doland. Of course, I don't know any of them, but . . ."

"They're OK. Jackie and Grant are pretty good guys. At least they used to be. . . . To tell you the truth, I don't hang around with them much anymore." He shook his head. "They spend too much time getting wasted. I'm just not into that."

Becka smiled, relieved.

Mike shrugged. "It didn't used to be so bad. Drugs and booze were just a once-in-a-while thing. But lately, it seems like they use them more and more to tune everything out. I'm afraid most of it has to do with Doland."

"What's he like?"

"Doland . . . he's pretty gone. Way over the edge. I think Jackie and Grant know it, too, but no one wants to confront him."

"Why not?"

"For one thing, he's the leader of the band. As lead singer, he's the one everybody knows.

His voice is a big part of our sound. . . . Without him, there would be no band. And also
. . . well, he's really hard to talk to these days. He just wants to do what he wants and nothing else."

"Sounds like my brother." Becka grinned.

Mike laughed again, which made her feel glad. Whenever Doland's name was brought up, Mike seemed so troubled. It felt good to see him smile again. "No, Scott's not like Doland," Mike continued. "Believe me."

"I don't know," Becka answered. "He sure wants his way all the time."

"Everyone's like that," Mike said, "especially toward their brother or sister. I know. I've got three sisters, and they all drive me crazy."

Again they both laughed. Becka was beginning to like this guy, and she could tell that he liked her. She shoved aside a momentary thought of Ryan back home. "When did you see them last? Your family, I mean."

Mike looked sad again. "It's been a couple of years, ever since I dropped out of college. I didn't even finish my first year. My sisters live in Arizona with my folks. My dad and I . . . we . . . we don't get along too well."

"What's the problem?"

"Lots of stuff," Mike said. "He wants everything on the straight and narrow, and I'm just not wired that way. I like to experiment, to do different things. He likes everything in a box, nice and neat. His career, his family . . . and especially his son."

"I guess that could be hard," Becka agreed. "But I'm sure he still loves you."

Mike glanced up, clearly surprised at her remark. "Yeah . . . I suppose. But we can't live together, I can tell you that. I never could live up to his expectations."

"Why did Doland ask you if we were from your dad's church?"

Mike sighed. "Before my dad retired, he was a pastor. Doland likes giving me a hard time about it."

Becka frowned. "What's he got against pastors—or churches?"

Mike looked out the window of the café for a moment before answering. "What's Tommy Doland got against pastors and churches? Nothing . . . except that he worships the devil."

In a dimly lit hotel room, Tommy Doland sat at a table, holding hands with three other people. A black candle sat in the middle of the table. A large bald man with a short black beard began to chant softly. "Darkness and shadow hold back the light; darkness and shadow hold back the light."

Doland and the other two people quietly

took up the chant: "Darkness and shadow hold back the light; darkness and shadow hold back the light."

The chanting lasted several minutes, growing louder and louder until it filled the room . . . until it filled their minds and bodies. "Darkness and shadow hold back the light; darkness and shadow hold back the light."

Finally, the leader raised his arms. The others fell silent and followed suit. Then the leader called out in a loud voice, "Overlord of the Western Hemisphere, Demon Prince of the city, what do you wish us to do with the intruder? What fate do you decree for the one who dares to challenge your authority over this carefully groomed project? What would you have us do with this person who has come to undermine our brother's efforts? What do you decree for Rebecca Williams?"

There was no response. Only silence. Then an unmistakable chill filled the room.

Suddenly the leader started to shake. The sound coming from him started as a deep rumble but grew into a vicious snarl. Doland's hands broke out into a sweat, but he kept his eyes clenched tight, continuing to concentrate.

Slowly the snarl evolved into a voice—a terrifying, guttural voice. As it spoke, the flame on the candle in the center of the

table began to waver. Suddenly, the voice
screamed four words that reverberated
through the room for a long, long time:
   "DEATH TO THE GIRL!"

6

As soon as she returned from lunch, Becka asked Scott if she could use his laptop to contact Z.

"Wait until I get back, and I'll do it," Scott suggested.

"No, you'll be gone for a couple of hours. I need to talk to him now."

Scott hesitated. "I don't know. It isn't mine, you know. It's Darryl's, and he'd be pretty mad if you messed with it."

Becka sighed. "I'm not going to play football with it, goofball! I just want to contact Z and ask him some questions about what Mike told me."

"All right," Scott said, handing her the laptop. "It's still got about an hour left on the charge, so you don't even need to plug it in."

"Thanks," Becka said, already typing on the keyboard.

"Whoa," Scott said, looking at his watch. "I'm supposed to be downstairs meeting Mike. Hope he holds the limo for me. See ya later."

"Bye . . . Oh, Scott, stay away from Doland. I'm afraid he might be—"

But Scott was already out the door.

～

Scott bounded out of the elevator and into the lobby, where he could see the limo waiting. "Cool!" he shouted a little too loudly for the somewhat reserved atmosphere of the Regent Beverly Wilshire Hotel. Running also was frowned upon. Scott forced himself to slow to a fast walk as he headed toward the door.

"Hey! Where's the fire?" a voice called out behind him. Scott turned around to see Mike.

"Didn't think we'd leave without you, did you?" Mike continued.

"Uh, n-no," Scott stammered. "But who is 'we'?"

"Well . . ." Mike hesitated. "Doland wants to check out the effects unit. They repaired it after last night."

Scott was caught off guard. "Doland? But I thought—"

Mike cut him off. "Hey, Doland! Meet the newest member of our crew."

Scott hadn't noticed Doland sitting near the door. The guy looked like his mind was a thousand miles away as he stood up to meet them.

"Doland," Mike said again as they reached the door, "this is Scott Williams. He's going to help us get ready for the show."

Suddenly Doland's eyes came into focus. His gaze was intense. "Hello, Scott."

Scott swallowed nervously. "Hi . . . Tommy." He didn't feel right calling Tommy Doland by the more familiar "Doland" like Mike did. He was relieved that Doland didn't seem to recognize him from last night's party.

But as they headed out of the hotel entrance, Doland turned and said, "So where's your babe of a sister today? Upstairs? In your room . . . I presume?"

He said the last phrase in a singsong voice, as if it were a rhyme he'd made up especially for the occasion. Scott could only stare, still nervous that Doland might remember him.

Doland said nothing, obviously waiting for an answer.

Finally, Scott said, "Yeah . . . I guess. She was using my laptop to contact . . ." He'd almost said Z but figured it was none of Doland's business. Why should he tell Doland anything?

Doland smiled that twisted smile of his. "Using your laptop, huh? Guess that's the story—A to *Z*."

He emphasized the *Z*. With a cold chill, Scott wondered if it was just a coincidence or if Doland had somehow read his mind.

~

Becka had no problem getting through to Z, thanks to the instant message system. She quickly filled Z in on what had happened so far, especially about her conversation with Mike.

What can I do to help Mike?

She waited a few moments. Suddenly, Z's reply came across the screen.

Get him away from Tommy Doland.

At first Becka figured she'd miscommunicated something. So she tried again.

*How can we do that? Doland's the
lead singer of the band.*

Z's answer was typically honest and straight
to the point.

Doland has willingly given himself over to
the devil. He will keep Mike from the
spiritual truth he needs.

Becka sat there, puzzled. Slowly, she typed:

*How can I ask Mike to quit the biggest
thing in his life?*

The answer returned quickly.

In Matthew 16:26 Jesus said, "How do you
benefit if you gain the whole world but lose your
own soul in the process? Is anything worth more
than your soul?" Without Christ, there is no life.
Everything else will pass away.

Becka nodded. Z was right; she knew it.
But his being right didn't make her task any
easier. She typed:

The Scream is the hottest band in the country.

Of course she knew there was no compari-
son between a hot band and the God of the

universe, but she didn't know if she could get that across to Mike. For a moment she wondered if Z would even bother replying. But the response soon came.

> Better to be the least within the kingdom of God than the greatest without.

Finally, Becka typed out her greatest concern:

> If Mike's father, a pastor, couldn't reach him, how can I?

The response was swift.

> Maybe you can't, but you should try.

Becka answered:

> But how? Maybe after we've known each other for a while, sure. But not yet.

Z's response appeared on the screen, filling Becka with dread.

> Mike does not have that much time.

Becka remembered her dream of the fiery cannon and was suddenly terrified for her new friend. But before she could type anything else, Z's final words appeared.

Must go. Do your best. And be careful. The devil
knows our weaknesses and uses them against us.
Remember that people are praying for you.
Z

Becka didn't fully understand the last part.
Suddenly, she felt so overwhelmed that she
didn't care what Z meant. Instead, she did
what she usually did when overwhelmed.
She prayed. She guessed that Z had referred
to Mike's family when he said that a lot of
people were praying. She figured it wouldn't
hurt to add one more to that number.

Scott was amazed at how much bigger the
auditorium looked when no one was there.
"It's like you could put the whole town of
Crescent Bay in here!"

Mike smiled, then turned to a scraggly-
looking guy with a bandaged hand and
several sores on his face. "Scott, this is Billy
Phelps. He's our stage manager. He got hurt
at the San Francisco concert. But he's doing
better now, right, Billy?"

Billy grinned. "Right."

"He'll show you what you need to do,"
Mike finished.

"Hey, Scott," Billy drawled with a slight
Southern accent, "you ready to rock?"

Scott shrugged. "Yeah . . . I guess."

Billy nodded. "All right. You can start with that bucket of empty whiskey bottles over there."

Scott turned to see a large tub filled with empty bottles.

"Take 'em over to that sink back there, and wash 'em out real good."

Scott nodded. "OK. Then what?"

"Then come see me. I'll be tinkering with the lights somewhere around the stage. Get me when you're done, and we'll fill 'em up."

"OK," Scott agreed, wondering why they wanted to reuse the bottles. *Oh, well,* he thought. *Guess it doesn't matter. I'm now part of the world of rock. Awesome!*

~

Doland watched the boy talking to Billy and Mike, feeling the rage build inside of him. He leaned over the control panel at the edge of the stage. So Rebecca Williams sent her brother into the battle, did she? Well, that was just fine. He could handle them both. And handle them he would.

~

After setting the sound levels for the drums, Mike quickly returned to the hotel to pick up Becka for a tour of the city. She had wanted to see a bit more of Los Angeles, and he had wanted to spend more time with her.

Now they stood at the famous intersection of Hollywood and Vine and looked up at the Capitol Records tower just down the street. When Becka looked to the left, she could just make out Mann's Chinese Theater, where the handprints of all the great stars—everyone from Clark Gable and Marilyn Monroe to Jack Nicholson and Michelle Pfeiffer—were encased in cement.

It should've been an exhilarating experience, but it wasn't. The Hollywood of old was long gone. Off to Becka's right were overpriced souvenir shops and topless bars. The street was busy all right, but no movie stars were to be seen. Instead, the sidewalks were filled with drug addicts and prostitutes. There were tourists here and there, but there were far more homeless people present. And it cut Becka to the quick to see many kids her age—and some even younger—among them. Young people from around the country had come out to Hollywood thinking they'd escape their boring hometown lives . . . only to find themselves caught up in an urban nightmare. For them, the street of dreams was nothing but a street of pain.

She felt a sense of relief when they headed for the limo. Mike had the driver take them past the fancy mansions of Beverly Hills and then out to the Venice Beach Boardwalk.

The afternoon was growing more perfect by the moment.

They hadn't talked much about The Scream. Becka was anxious to ask more questions after what she'd learned from Z, but she suspected the subject would upset Mike. She didn't want to do that. Everything was too perfect.

Half an hour later they were having ice-cream sundaes at an outdoor shop in the Century City mall. The big office building towered over them. The mall was crowded with busy executives.

"See that guy over there?" Mike nodded to the right.

Becka turned to see a short man dressed in an expensive business suit, Italian sunglasses perched on his nose, walking hurriedly through the mall. Three taller men wearing similar suits and sunglasses tried their best to keep up with him.

"That's Jason Unger, the agent," Mike said. "Some people think he's the most powerful guy in the entertainment business."

"Who are the other three guys?"

"Dunno. Underlings probably. He's got a zillion of them, or so they say."

"Do they all try to dress like he does?"

"Sure," Mike said. "And walk and talk like he does, too."

Becka laughed. "That's crazy."

"You got that right," Mike said with a grin. "Now, what do you want to do next?"

"Watch the sunset from the ocean," Becka said before she could catch herself.

Mike smiled. "All right—one sunset coming up. But after that, I need to get you back to the hotel. I told your mom we wouldn't be out too late."

It wasn't until they were back in the limo, heading toward Zuma Beach, that Becka finally worked up the courage to talk about the band. "Mike . . . can I ask you something?"

Mike nodded. "Shoot."

"What are you going to do about the band?"

He looked puzzled. "Do? What do you mean?"

"Well, I was thinking about what you said about Doland—about his worshiping the devil and stuff. Doesn't that worry you?"

Mike sighed and looked off into the distance. "Well, I used to think it was an act with Doland . . . but not anymore. Sometimes it doesn't bother me at all. Other times . . ."

"What?" she prodded.

"Well, sometimes, like when everyone makes a big fuss over us . . . sometimes that bothers me."

"Why? I mean, you've worked hard for it."

"Yeah, we're pretty good. But there are lots of good bands. Sometimes I just . . . I guess I feel funny about the band's success, because I'm not sure where it came from."

Becka gulped. She had a hunch where this was going.

Mike continued, "In the beginning, the black magic and devil stuff were more of a gimmick than anything we believed in. We even used to make fun of it. But it kept growing somehow. And then . . . it just got out of control, especially with Doland. Now it's like the band isn't even in charge anymore."

"What do you mean?"

Mike shrugged, looking uncomfortable as the limo pulled into the beach parking lot. "I don't know. I'm probably just superstitious. All the guys say I am."

"That's just because you believe in something—" Becka stopped in midsentence, not sure if this was the right thing to say— "or . . . at least you *did* believe in something . . . at one time."

Mike laughed. "Yeah, I guess that's one way of putting it."

Two minutes later, they were sitting on the hood of the limo, watching the sun sink into the ocean. Becka could not have asked for a better day. A great lunch, a tour of L.A. in a limo, and now a perfect sunset beside a great guy.

She took a deep breath and slowly let it

out. "This is so beautiful," she said. "I always try to take time to watch the sunsets at home."

"I bet it's even prettier where you live," Mike said.

"I don't know. It all depends on where you are at the moment."

Mike turned and looked into her eyes. "And who you're seeing it with?"

Becka felt her stomach flip-flop. A warmth rushed to her cheeks. "Yeah . . . that, too."

He hesitated a moment longer before leaning toward her. She leaned forward too, certain that he wanted to kiss her. Then at the last second she blurted out, "So, are you going to tell me what you meant when you said that the band wasn't in charge anymore?"

Mike stopped and looked at her. "You sure have a strange way of communicating sometimes, Rebecca Williams."

She smiled nervously.

Mike turned to stare at the sunset again. "All I meant was that sometimes things feel so out of control that it's like . . . it's as if someone, or some*thing,* else is calling the shots. I don't know. . . . I think Doland is into some pretty weird stuff and . . . somehow that affects all of us."

"Then why don't you quit?"

Mike laughed. "Are you serious?"

Becka nodded. "Sure, if it's the only way you'll be free of Doland."

"Quit the band?!" Mike's voice carried an edge of irritation. "No way! I worked my whole life for this. I'm *never* quitting the band."

Becka felt miserable. "Look, I'm sorry. I didn't mean to upset you. It's just that . . . well . . . I've seen people fool around with demonic stuff . . . and it can get pretty dangerous. I mean, something awful could happen . . . and I . . ."

He was looking at her again. For a moment she forgot what she was saying. She tried again. ". . . I don't want anything . . ."

He leaned toward her.

". . . awful to happen to . . ."

His lips found hers. For an instant, Becka melted. She kissed him back. Mike's arms came around her, holding her close. Becka knew she should pull away. For an instant, she thought of Ryan back home. How would she feel if he kissed another girl? Then came the thought of a promise she had once made to Mom about never letting herself get into a compromising situation with a boy.

Yet, in spite of all that, she let the kiss continue. It grew in intensity until all she could think of was *Mike, Mike, Mike. . . .*

Then another thought came to mind: *The devil knows our weaknesses and uses them against us.*

She suddenly stiffened. Mustering all of her will, she pulled away.

Mike looked at her, confused. She could also tell that he seemed a little hurt.

She wanted to explain herself but didn't know if she could. The attraction between them had been surprisingly strong. Was this the weakness Z had warned her about— something the enemy would use against her? Part of her knew that when a person dealt with the supernatural, things were rarely what they seemed.

She let out a small breath of air. "I . . . uh . . . I need to get back," she finally managed. "Mom will be worrying."

Mike slowly exhaled. "Sure . . . I probably need to check in with the guys anyway. We've gotta iron out the final plans for tomorrow's telecast. It's the biggest thing for us yet . . . a national broadcast. . . . It's gonna be a real blast."

Becka nodded. But as they slid off the hood and climbed back into the limo, all she could think about was her dream from the night before—the one with the cannon exploding—and Mike's words: *"It's gonna be a real blast."*

7

The next morning Becka tried to contact Z again. She wanted Scott to join her, but he was too busy listening to the latest Scream CD through his headphones. "If I'm gonna be part of the band, I need to be more familiar with their music!" he shouted.

"You're *not* part of the band!" Becka shouted back. "You're just helping them set up for one show!"

Scott removed the headphones. "That's all *you* know. First of all, when we in showbiz refer to the 'band,' we mean the entire organization that makes the thing happen. The agents, producers, label execs, manager, road manager, and crew. That last part includes me. As for this being my only show, Billy already said that he wished he had someone like me around all the time."

Becka shrugged. "So?"

"So that's exactly the kind of thing they say before they offer you a regular gig."

Becka tried not to laugh. "A regular gig? Don't you think you ought to finish high school first?"

Scott pointed his index finger at Becka and then flipped his hand over in a quick gesture.

"What does that mean?" she said. "Or do I want to know?"

"It means, 'Have it *your* way, burger brain.' It's a band thing. Billy does it whenever the hall manager or the security guys hassle him. I think it's pretty cool."

Becka sighed. "I think it's pretty stupid. You've only been working for them one day, and you're already all caught up in this . . . band stuff."

"You're so uncool, Becka."

"And you're even more of an idiot than usual."

"I am *not* more of an idiot!" Scott snapped as he put the headphones back on. "I'm just the same as I've always been!"

Becka shook her head in amusement as she turned back to the computer. She wanted to talk with Z, to tell him that he'd been right about the enemy using her weaknesses against her. She was falling for the guy she was supposed to be helping. And instead of making things better, she was afraid she was only making matters worse.

Then there was Scott. He was getting caught up in the glamour of the band's fame—all the glitz and the hype. Yessir, there was definitely a battle going on. It was one they'd never fought before. Instead of in-your-face warfare, everything seemed cool and glamorous. In fact, when she thought about it that way, she realized that the weapons being used against them in this encounter were actually more dangerous than in some of the other fights they had faced. In this encounter, all of the enemy's weapons were things they wanted.

As the e-mail symbol on the laptop flashed, Becka clicked on it, then opened up the incoming message. But it wasn't from Z. It was from Ryan.

Hey, Beck! Hope you guys are doing OK. I miss you a lot, but I guess I have to learn to put my needs

*aside when you're doing important stuff like this.
Who knows what good effect this kind of thing can
have on others. I guess that's the great thing
about being a Christian. All we have to do is say
yes to God, and he does the rest. All you and
Scott had to do was be willing to go to L.A. Now
God's leading you step-by-step the rest of the way.
I just wanted to let you know that I'm praying for
you guys, and I can't wait until you get back—
Especially you, Beck. Love, Ryan*

It was all Becka could do to swallow the
lump in her throat. Ryan was the closest
thing to a boyfriend she had ever had. And
though she still didn't feel comfortable with
that term, he had always treated her wonder-
fully. Now here he was, trying to encourage
her to let God use her to help others. She
had practically dumped him for some guy
she hardly even knew! If she had felt bad
about kissing Mike before, she felt terrible
about it now.

And it was these exact feelings that helped
her decide what to do next. "Scott," she
called, "I want to go to rehearsal with you
today." But Scott was in his own world with
the headphones on and his eyes closed.

"He can't hear you with those things on,"
Mom said as she passed by. "You'll have to
get his attention."

Becka agreed. Seeing a pencil eraser on

the table nearby, she grabbed it and threw it at him, hitting him square in the forehead.

Scott's eyes popped open. He glared at her. "Hey! What was that for?" he demanded, jerking off his headphones.

"I was just trying to get your attention."

"Why didn't you just use a club?"

"I couldn't find one," she countered. "Listen, I want to go to rehearsal with you today."

"We're not rehearsing. We're recording," Scott replied. "You'll just get in the way."

Becka shook her head. "I'm going, because I need to talk to Mike. What time are they sending the car?"

"Two o'clock," Scott replied. "But you'd better not bother Mike when he's recording."

"He won't get mad at me," Becka said confidently.

"It's not Mike I'm worried about. Doland's the one who'll get upset. He doesn't like distractions."

Becka paused, and for the briefest second she considered not going. Her stomach was already churning. The last thing she wanted was a confrontation with Doland. In fact, she dreaded seeing Doland at all.

But she had to go.

～

The band had left earlier, so Scott and Becka were the only ones in the limo that afternoon.

Scott wore his best torn T-shirt and torn jeans. In fact, they were *new* torn jeans.

"Scott, are those your new jeans?" Becka asked incredulously. "Tell me you didn't tear holes in your new jeans."

"Don't tell Mom, OK?"

"I won't have to. She'll figure that out for herself. Don't you think you're taking this band thing a little too far?"

Scott scowled and looked out the window. Even though they teased each other constantly, they had always been close. They had to be after all they'd been through together. But something was happening to Becka's little brother. In the past forty-eight hours he had begun to slip away—growing more and more distant, more and more into himself. She knew that the change in his behavior was because of the band's influence—and the subtle deception he was buying into. She also knew that if she brought it up, he wouldn't listen.

There was, however, Someone who *would* listen.

God, please remind Scotty of your truth, she prayed. *I know he believes in you. But sometimes, others influence him. . . . And Lord, please protect us. It feels like we're in over our heads with this assignment. I know you told us in the Bible that when we're weak, you're strong. Well, we've sure got plenty of weaknesses this time! Please be there for us. Show us what to do. Amen.*

As soon as they climbed out of the car, the limo drove off, leaving them standing outside a plain-looking brick building. "Are you sure this is the place?" Becka asked. "It looks like a warehouse."

"This is the address Billy gave me," Scott said. "I think they like to keep it low-key on the outside so people won't know about all the expensive equipment inside."

The door was locked, and a small sign said Ring Buzzer. Becka pushed the buzzer. Nothing happened.

"Maybe we should've called first," Scott said after a minute.

Suddenly they heard a whirring sound. Looking up, they saw a small camera tucked away under the awning. As it slowly turned, the lens moved.

"Wow. That's a pretty high-tech security camera," Becka said. "They're checking us out. Wonder who's on the other end."

"Probably some jerk," Scott said.

Then a voice from out of nowhere said, "Watch who you're calling a jerk, jerk!"

Scott blushed. "They can *hear* us!"

The voice spoke again. "Right you are, loser. Lucky I know you're smarter than you look."

"It's Billy!" Scott exclaimed.

"Right again," the voice said. "Come on in."

With that he buzzed the door open. Inside, the place was completely different than it looked from the outside. They entered a large reception area with walls of sleek black marble and a thick, plush black carpet. The walls were covered with silver and platinum records in black metal frames. On them were names like Pearl Jam, Alanis Morissette, Aerosmith, Petra, and Boys II Men.

"Wow!" Scott said. "Look at this. All these people recorded here!"

Becka was also impressed. "Hey, here's Jars of Clay. I love that band."

In the center of the room was a large black marble reception desk. To the left of the desk, three monitors displayed images from the security cameras at the three entrances to the building. A fancy phone system and an expensive-looking PC perched on the desk to the right. And behind all of this expensive, high-tech equipment sat the scraggly Billy Phelps.

"Howdy." Billy grinned. "Pretty cool place, eh?"

"I'll say," Scott replied. "Where are the guys?"

Billy pointed down the hallway. "Studio B. They're doing overdubs. But I brought some of your work with me."

"Work?" Scott asked.

Billy pointed toward a large tub of empty whiskey bottles and a couple of plastic jugs full of an amber liquid. Scott nodded.

Becka cleared her throat. "Excuse me. . . . I came to see Mike."

Billy nodded. "I figured. You're Rebecca, right? They're in the middle of a take right now, but I'll get word to them in a minute that you're here."

Becka thanked him and crossed to where Scott filled the empty bottles. "What are you doing?"

"Yesterday Billy had me wash out these whiskey bottles. Today he wants me to fill them."

"Is that whiskey?" Becka interrupted, pointing to the plastic jugs from which Scott was filling the bottles.

"No," Scott replied. "That's just it. It's iced tea."

"Iced tea? Why would they want . . . ? Oh, I get it."

Scott waited, but Becka said nothing. Finally, he sighed, "Well, then, explain it to me, will you?"

Becka shook her head in sad amusement. "Don't you get it? They want to strut around onstage, guzzling from these whiskey bottles like it doesn't bother them . . . which it doesn't, since the bottles are really just full of iced tea."

"Can't give a good performance when you're drunk," Billy Phelps said, walking up behind them. "You can go in now, Rebecca.

Right down the hall. Only make sure you don't enter when the red light is on."

~

As Becka headed down the hall, Scott turned to Billy. "I still don't get this whiskey thing," he said. "Why do the guys want people to think they're drinking a lot when they're not?"

"Part of the image, kid. The crowd expects that from a heavy-metal band. Part of the whole heavy-metal mystique."

"What about the kids out there who think they should be imitating them by guzzling down booze?"

"Oh, well." Billy grinned.

Scott frowned. He didn't much like the answer.

"This stuff is big business, kid. Too much money on the line to blow something because of a few drinks."

"Doesn't sound very real to me," Scott said.

"It's not about real, Scott," Billy said. "It's about money."

~

Becka walked down a hall also lined with gold and platinum records. On the left was a large, airtight, wooden door. Becka started to grab the handle, then stopped when she noticed the red light glowing above the door.

Several seconds later, it turned off. She quickly entered the dimly lit studio.

Mike, Jackie, and Grant stood near a long recording console just a few feet away. It looked like the equalizer section on Scott's stereo, except it was about fifty times larger. Behind the board sat a bushy-haired guy with glasses. He turned and tweaked various knobs as he listened with the others to the playback of a vocal Doland had just recorded. Through a big picture window she could see Doland, listening to the playback from the vocal booth.

As soon as she entered, Mike smiled and nodded to her. Becka grinned back. She instinctively pulled away from the window to a spot where Doland could not see her.

"You guys are acting like a bunch of wimps about this fire-cannon thing!" Doland shouted at the rest of the band through the monitor speakers. "We're letting the fans down. They come expecting a wild ride. That means the whole ball of wax—fireworks and pushing the envelope."

"Sure," Jackie spoke to him through the intercom. "But we've gotta have this stuff double- and triple-checked. I'm not spending my life in jail because this stupid cannon of yours takes some guy's arm off in the tenth row."

Becka felt her stomach tighten. They were

talking about the cannon—the same one that had nearly killed Mike earlier; the same one, only smaller, that she had dreamed about. The image of Mike's burned face and charred lips screaming in agony was so vivid that for a moment Becka actually thought she saw the scene before her. She closed her eyes, and it went away. Unfortunately, the topic of the cannon did not.

"The cannon will be fine. I told you that. Billy looked at it. It'll be fine."

"What was wrong with it?" Mike asked.

"It came loose, all right?" Doland griped. "That stuff happens!"

"What about the night Billy got hurt?" Mike persisted. "What was wrong with it then?"

"I don't know!" Doland was getting more and more angry. "I'm not an expert on cannons. I just don't want to wimp out for the big show, that's all. We're talking national TV here, dudes. A forty-million-plus audience. Our biggest show ever!"

"All right, all right!" Jackie raised his hands. "Let's keep the cannon in."

Grant, the bass player, reluctantly nodded. It was clear that Mike didn't agree. What was equally clear was that he had just been out-voted.

That decision settled, they went back to the music.

"That last take was great, Tommy." The

bushy-haired producer behind the recording board spoke into his talk-back microphone. "But I'd like to try another one if you can. Try holding back a bit on the second chorus so that it makes more of an impact on the last chorus when you cut loose."

"You want *more* on the last chorus?" Doland's voice through the monitor speakers definitely sounded offended.

"No, no," the producer replied. "I want the same there . . . just soften the second chorus so that the last one stands out more."

"That's what I said!" Doland snapped. "You want *more* on the last chorus! Just roll the tape, dude."

"OK," the producer said, doing his best to keep the peace. "We're rolling."

As the song began, Mike took the opportunity to step over to Becka. "Hi," he whispered.

She smiled. "I hope I'm not interrupting anything."

"No, no. Doland just wants to sweeten up some of the vocals."

"Will he mind that I'm here?"

Mike shook his head. "With the bright lighting in his booth and the dim light in here, he can't even see you. Is everything OK?"

Becka took a breath. "Well . . . yes and no." *Here goes,* she thought. "Mike, I really have gotten to like you in these past few

days, and I hope we stay friends for a long
time, but—"

"Whoa!" Mike cut her off. "It's the 'let's
just be friends' speech? Already? I didn't
expect that for at least another week."

Becka smiled. "Sorry, Mike. It's just
that there's this boy back home that I like
and . . ."

"And what?"

"And . . . well, I sort of got carried away
last night on the beach with the sunset and
all . . . and . . . you. I was letting my emotions
get the better of me."

"Some people call that love, Becka," Mike
said.

Even in the dim light, she could see his
softened expression. For a moment Becka
began to weaken. But Z's message coupled
with Ryan's strengthened her. She continued, "I suppose, but I call it . . . well, I call
it losing control. I mean, I'm flattered and
everything, but I know what I want now,
and . . . this isn't it."

A slight frown crossed Mike's face.

"Don't get me wrong," Becka continued.
"It's attractive, but . . . I just, I just don't
think I'm ready for a serious relationship."

"What do you call what you have with the
dude back home?"

"We're friends," Becka answered. "Well,
actually, a little more than friends. It's grow-

ing, but it's at a slow pace. And that's the way I like it."

"Does this mean you're not coming to the TV concert tonight?"

"I was hoping to, unless you'd prefer me not to come. I *do* consider you a friend, Mike. I suppose that sounds stupid, but I really do care for you that way. And . . ." She hesitated, unsure if she should go on, but knowing she had to. "I've been worrying about you a lot."

"Me?" He looked surprised.

She nodded, but before she could continue, Doland started singing. Everyone suddenly grew very quiet.

The lyrics had barely started before Becka felt that all-too-familiar chill running across her shoulders.

But it was more than just his voice that caused her to react.

As Mike said, because the lights in the control room were much dimmer than in Doland's vocal booth, there was no way that Doland could see her. Yet as he sang, his eyes seemed to focus directly upon her. Gradually they filled with more and more hatred. They bore into her . . . and definitely scared her.

The song continued to build. Now Doland seemed to be going into some sort of trance. Becka had seen similar expressions like that before—too many times during encounters with demons. If she had doubted before that Doland had turned the control of his life over to someone or something, she was sure of it now. And whatever that something was, Becka was equally sure it was not good.

A better word would be *evil.*

Soon Becka found herself doing what she always did when she became afraid. She silently prayed. But this time, she didn't utter a prayer for help. Instead, she quietly worshiped as a reminder to herself of God's great power. *Thank you, Lord. Thank you for your love, for your awesome—*

She had barely started, when Doland suddenly screamed. It was a hideous, terrifying sound that was more animal than human— one that hinted of deep rage and pain.

The producer scrambled to stop the tape. "Tommy! What's wrong?"

Even stronger chills ran through Becka as Doland suddenly pointed at her. His voice was low and guttural. *"Get her out of here!"*

"Who?" the producer asked. "Get who out, Tommy?"

Doland glared maniacally. *"Get her out now!"*

Becka looked up at Mike. Her mouth was bone dry. "He means me."

"But he can't even see you! How could he—?"

"Trust me, Mike. He means me. Can we

talk somewhere? It's really important that we talk."

"Sure. Let's go into the hall." As soon as they stepped into the hallway, he looked down at her intently. "What happened in there? How'd he know you were there?"

Becka took a deep breath and slowly let it out. "Mike . . . I think Doland's under some kind of . . . I think the devil has a stronghold inside of him."

"Whoa." Mike held up his hand. "Doland's weird and all, but he's not . . . possessed. I mean, I know the guy's a jerk, but—"

"He went nuts just now because I was praying."

Mike looked at her strangely. "Praying?"

Becka nodded. "I was praying when he went crazy."

"Don't be silly," Mike said. "Doland didn't know you were praying. He just doesn't like strangers there."

"But he couldn't see me. You said so yourself."

The reply caught Mike off guard. "Look, I know Doland's weird sometimes, but—"

"Doland is more than weird. You know that better than I do. You said he was into devil worship." She held his gaze, and after swallowing again, said, "It's dangerous for you here, Mike. You know the truth. You know what Doland's about. And if you keep refusing—"

"Look, Rebecca." Mike cut her off. There was no missing the anger in his voice. "If you don't want to go out with me, fine. But don't preach to me."

Suddenly Doland threw open the door to the studio. "What is *she* doing here?!"

"She's . . . she's my friend," Mike said.

Doland yelled loud enough for the rest of the band to hear. "I'm out of here until Mike's through messing around with the chicks! I'll be in the bar next door!"

He started toward Becka. She braced herself, but he did not touch her. Still, even as he passed, his glare was so intense that she found herself taking a step back.

Something evil was at work there. She knew it beyond the shadow of a doubt.

8

Doland stormed
out of the studio, letting the door slam
behind him.

Mike looked at the floor and slowly shook
his head. "Well, that about does it for today.
I'd say his concentration is definitely blown."
He turned to Becka. "Listen, you want a ride
back to the hotel?"

"What about Scotty?"

"What about me?" Scott asked as he strolled
up with Billy and Jackie.

"We'll take him home," Billy offered.

Becka hesitated. "OK . . . I guess we'll see you back at the hotel, then."

"Sounds good to me," Scott said. Without another word, he turned and followed Billy and Jackie out the door.

As soon as they were in the parking lot, Jackie turned to Scott and asked, "Are you coming to the broadcast party?"

"Sure," Scott said without thinking. "Where is it?"

"House up in the hills," Jackie replied. "Starts in a couple of hours. It'll probably be a little wild."

Scott knew that he shouldn't go. Something felt wrong. He even thought about praying about that feeling. But the broadcast would begin in just a few hours. After that his job would be over. Tomorrow he would be back on the plane heading home. The band would just be a memory.

Before he could stop himself, he answered, "Sure, I'll be there." He tried to ignore the prickly feeling at the back of his mind that seemed to grow stronger.

~

In Mike's limo on the way home, Becka said another silent prayer. It was time to bring up the subject of the band again. This time she hoped that Mike would understand. "Mike

. . . I . . . I want you to know something. It's only because I care about you that . . . that I think it's important for you to think about leaving the band."

Mike's eyes flashed anger. "You sound just like my father when you say that."

"Don't you think your father cares about you?"

"Sure he cares about me. But he wants to control my every move, too."

"Isn't that just because he loves you?"

"You don't know him."

"No, I don't. But I do know that God still loves you."

Mike made a face. "Please . . ."

"Mike, don't confuse your feelings about your dad with your feelings about Jesus. Your father may have been a pastor, but he wasn't perfect. Christ's love is perfect. Don't turn your back on him."

Mike sighed. "I suppose now you're going to tell me that Jesus wants me to quit the band, too?"

"Do you think Jesus wants you to sing songs that give glory to Satan?"

Mike shook his head. "Becka, that's just part of the show!"

As the car pulled into the hotel's parking lot, she turned and looked him straight in the eyes. "Even you don't believe that."

He glanced away.

"Besides, why *pretend* to like the devil just to sell records? How do you think that affects your fans?"

"Look, Rebecca—" Mike's voice was cool and even—"I used to think you cared about me. Now I'm not so sure. I don't know what the deal is, but—"

"Mike—"

He cut her off with an angry shake of his head. "Hey, if you don't want to go out with me, that's cool with me! That's your business! But I'll live my life my way! I don't need your preaching!"

His words stung Becka. She had tried every argument she knew. Nothing had worked. She was sad, frustrated, and mad. OK, fine! If he didn't want to listen, if he didn't want her help, that was *his* business. She threw the limo door open and stepped out. "If that's the way you want it, Mike Parsek, then that's the way you'll have it!"

She slammed the door and stalked toward the hotel. She could feel his eyes on her. A moment later she heard the limo squeal off down the driveway.

～

When Becka returned to the suite, she snapped on the computer. A message awaited her.

"Mom," she asked, "has Scotty seen this?"

Mom shook her head. "I don't think so, dear. He's been in the shower for quite a while."

Becka nodded and clicked on the message. It was from Z.

Rebecca: Don't throw the baby out with the bathwater. Contact me as soon as possible.

Z

Becka frowned. "What does that mean?"

"What does what mean, honey?" Mom asked from across the room.

"'Don't throw the baby out with the bathwater.'"

Mom laughed. "Oh, that's an old expression. Your father used to use it all the time. It means don't lose sight of the big picture."

Becka scowled as if she still didn't understand.

Mom smiled. "Sometimes people get so caught up with a little problem that they lose sight of the overall good. You know, like not seeing the forest for the trees."

Becka felt more confused than ever. "I sort of understood you until you got to the trees part. I think I'll just wait to see what Z says."

Mom nodded. "Sounds like a good idea."

"I have to talk to him anyway," Becka continued. "I've gotten nowhere with Mike.

The big TV concert is tonight, we go home tomorrow, and not a thing has changed."

"What do you mean?"

"It's obvious Mike should quit the band. I mean, Doland is so far gone he's practically growing horns. But Mike just won't see it. I'm afraid we've wasted Z's money and our time. So we might as well—"

She came to a stop as Scott emerged from the bathroom. First, there was the towel on his head, which, frankly, looked kind of stupid. Then, after he took the towel off, there was the shock of red hair sticking straight up from his forehead. Not red like a redhead— red like a fire engine.

"Scotty!" Mom half gasped, half shrieked. "Did you dye your hair?"

Scott fingered the rest of his brown locks. "Uh . . . yeah."

"Why?"

"I figured it would look cool." Scott tried to say it with a straight face, but Becka could tell that he was pretty mortified himself.

She did her best not to snicker, but it was a losing battle.

"What?!" Scott snapped. "What's wrong with it?"

"Nothing's wrong with it," Becka said, trying to hide her laugh with a cough, "if you're a rooster."

Anger struggled with humor on Scott's

face. Humor won out when he glanced at his reflection in a mirror. "I guess not everybody looks good in red," he said with a laugh.

"You march right back into the bathroom and wash that stuff out!" Mom ordered. Suddenly she looked a little scared. "It *does* wash out, doesn't it?"

"It's just Kool-Aid, Mom," he said. "Most of it will come out in one wash . . . unless you're a blond."

"Then go wash that Kool-Aid out of your hair this instant."

Scott headed back into the bathroom. This was one experiment that had obviously failed.

Becka said nothing more about Scott's hair until after he washed it and sat drying it vigorously with a towel. "You wanted to look like a rocker, didn't you?"

Scott stopped rubbing for a minute. "I wanted to look . . . different. Like somebody else besides plain ol' Scott."

Becka nodded. "I kinda went through that a few years ago."

Scott laughed. "You mean when you got that French haircut?"

"Yeah," Becka said, joining in the chuckle. "It did look pretty weird, didn't it?"

Scott shrugged. "Yeah." After another moment, he continued. "So . . . you and Mike are quits?"

"We're *friends*. That's the way it should be, don't you think?"

"Yeah." Scott nodded. "I mean, you can't forget about Ryan. He's pretty cool. But it was kinda cool to think I had a sister dating somebody famous."

Becka smiled in spite of herself. She grew serious moments later. "Scott, I'm worried. I think the band could destroy Mike. . . . By the way, I'm not sure it's doing wonders for you."

Scott shook his head. "You're way off base about the band, Beck. I know Doland's a little weird, but Jackie and Grant are OK. And Mike's cool."

Becka decided not to mince words. "Scott . . . Doland worships the devil. He's a satanist."

"No way!" Scott almost sounded hurt. "That's just an act! It's just so they can sell CDs!"

Becka shook her head. "It may have started out as an act, but it isn't anymore. And even if it is, think about it. They're pretending to like the devil just to sell more CDs. That's pretty sleazy, don't you think?"

Scott looked at her, then shrugged, as if to say that that was just her opinion. But Becka could tell by the way he clammed up that he was thinking things over.

"Scott!" Mom shouted the instant he

stopped drying his hair and let the towel fall around his neck. "Your hair . . . It's . . . it's yellow!"

Becka put her hand to her mouth in surprise, but a laugh still escaped. "I'd say it's kind of green, too."

Scott groaned. "Oh no!" Apparently the Kool-Aid wasn't as easy to wash out as he had thought.

Mom sprang into action. "Get your shirt on. We're going to the beauty parlor in the lobby to ask their advice."

"Mom . . . ," Scott complained. "That beauty parlor's for girls!"

"Sorry, Scott," Mom said as she handed him the shirt. "We've got no other choice!"

With another loud groan, Scott slipped on his shirt, resigned to his fate.

As soon as they left, Becka noticed the little *Z* blinking on Scott's computer. Maybe Z was calling her back. She crossed to the keyboard quickly.

9

With fingers flying across the keyboard, Becka carefully explained to Z what had happened with Mike. She then asked him to clarify his last message about the baby and the bathwater.

Z's reply was swift.

Many Christians think that members of a band like The Scream are not worth loving.

Becka quickly typed:

The guys in the band aren't bad. They're just
confused. Mike is cool though.

Z's response again was swift.

So why are you throwing him out
with the bathwater?

Becka suddenly felt guilty and didn't like it. She quickly shot back:

I told him to quit the band. It's not my fault
if he doesn't listen. Besides, he wanted
to go out with me. What about Ryan?

Z replied:

Are you angry at Mike or at yourself?

As Becka thought about that question, the memory of the evening she spent at Zuma Beach with Mike replayed itself in her mind. She slowly typed:

I shouldn't have let my guard down around him.
I think I was caught up in how I felt.

Z's next words gave Becka a sense of relief.

Wisdom is often gained at a price. You
have learned. Forgive yourself and move on.
Just because Mike is not the person who
should be your boyfriend doesn't mean he can't
be a boy who is also a friend.

Becka nodded as she read Z's reply, before
quickly explaining her growing fears for Scott.
Z replied:

You and Scott are doing what most Christians
do when confronted with a culture or group
activity that's new to them. They either want
nothing to do with it or the people who participate
in it (as in your case) or they get so involved that
they get caught up in it (like Scott).

Becka typed:

What do I do about Scotty?

Z replied:

Scott's clothes and hair are not the problem.
The question is, Is he compromising his beliefs?

Becka quickly typed:

How will I know?

Z answered:

Start by asking him. This evening will be your last chance to reach Mike. Be careful of Doland. And remember Ephesians 6:11: "Put on all of God's armor so that you will be able to stand firm against all strategies and tricks of the Devil."

Z

Becka signed off, her mind in a whirl. What could she do to help Mike? She had already told him that he should quit the band. What else could she say? She understood why it was hard for him to leave, but the more she recognized the growing evil, the more the pluses of leaving outweighed those of staying, no matter how popular the band was.

And then she heard it—a light scratching or rubbing sound that seemed to come from the bedroom she shared with Mom. She went into the room and turned on the light. Just as suddenly, the sound stopped.

It probably came from the next room, she thought. *I'll bet even in the best hotels you sometimes hear people laughing or making noise in the next room.*

Becka waited half a minute before she shut off the light and returned to the main room of the suite. As she flopped on the sofa, her mind drifted back to Mike. Maybe he didn't need to be told that he should give up the band. Instead of hearing what he *should* do, maybe he just needed to be reminded of God's great love for him.

Being a pastor's son didn't always mean having a perfect understanding of God's love. Sometimes pastors were so busy meeting other people's needs that their families ended up paying the price. Perhaps Mike did not receive all of the attention he needed. Maybe Mike had forgotten just how loved he was.

Scratch . . . scratch . . . scratch.

There it was again. The sound *was* coming from their bedroom. But as soon as Becka switched on the light, the sound stopped. *This is ridiculous,* she thought. But, ridiculous or not, the sound was driving her nuts . . . and making her a little afraid, too.

She decided to play a trick of her own. Once again she shut off the light and walked out of the room. Only this time, she tiptoed back in without turning on the light.

Scratch . . . scratch . . . scratch. Sure enough, the sound started again. *Scratch . . . scratch . . . scratch.* As she listened closely, she suddenly realized where the sound was coming from. It came from the door that connected their suite to the next one! Someone in the next room was trying to pick the lock!

Heart pounding, Becka made a dive for the phone to call the manager, then changed her mind and tiptoed toward the door leading out of the room. All she could think about was getting out of there! But before she could leave the room, she heard the lock click open.

Someone was coming inside!

She looked around, then quickly ducked into the closet, keeping the door open a crack. She suddenly wished that she and Mom had packed more clothes for better camouflage.

As she peered through the crack, she could see two men moving about the room. One was thin and scraggly looking with a mean face. The other was big, burly, and bald, with a small black beard. They quickly moved through the bedroom toward the main room of the suite. As they passed the closet, Becka could see that the burly man carried a large potato sack and the scraggly guy had some rope.

A cold wave of fear washed over her as she realized that they searched for her. They were planning to kidnap her!

Jesus, help me! she prayed.

"She ain't here," the scraggly guy called.

"Must have snuck out," the other grunted. "You think she heard us?"

"Maybe. We'd better get out of here in case she ran to get help."

"Let's go," the big man agreed. "We'll come back for her tonight when they're all asleep."

Becka heard the men go back through the connecting door and relock it. She waited for what felt like hours but could only have been minutes, praying and trying to calm herself. Finally, she opened the closet door and stepped out.

A sudden flash of light blinded her, while a deep voice shouted, "Get her!"

They had faked her out!

Becka tried to run, but big, meaty hands grabbed her. Another pair of hands slapped a large piece of tape over her mouth.

"Get that bag over her!" the deep voice commanded.

Becka felt the coarse potato sack burn her face as it dropped over her head. Then she felt ropes tied around her hands and the bag.

"Got her," the second voice said. "Doland said to take her to the warehouse."

"Right," the deep voice agreed. "We'll fry her there the same time Doland fries that drummer onstage."

Please help me, Jesus! Becka prayed frantically.

As rough hands grabbed her, she kicked and wriggled but could only move in short hops. She suddenly felt herself hoisted onto someone's shoulder.

Please, Jesus, please!

Just then, she heard the hall door open. Scott's voice called, "Wait'll you see this, Beck!"

She wanted to shout, but her mouth was sealed tight. She felt herself carried toward the connecting door.

"Beck, where are you?"

Suddenly the light came on in the bedroom. She heard Scott shout and the big man's voice yell, *"Run!"*

The next thing she knew she was dropped like . . . well, like a sack of potatoes. She heard the swift pounding of footsteps.

Moments later, a very frightened Scott pulled the bag from her face. "Beck, you all right?"

Becka nodded as Scott carefully removed the tape from her mouth. "We've gotta call the cops!" he exclaimed.

When the tape was gone, she gasped for air. "We've got . . . we've got to warn Mike! I heard them say Doland is planning on killing him."

"What? Say you're kidding me, Beck!"

Becka shook her head. As soon as Scott untied her, she tried to call Mike, but there was no answer from his room.

"Wait!" Scott said, looking at his watch. "He wouldn't be in his room now. He's at the broadcast party."

"Do you know where it is? We've gotta warn him!"

"Yeah. Jackie gave me the address . . . but . . . we'll have to take a cab. Mom's down-

stairs having her hair done. We need to call
the cops, too, to get after those guys that left!"

"There's no time to get Mom or the police!"
Becka snapped. "Leave her a note and let's get
outta here!"

~

Mike stared at the other band members,
trying to block out the sound of the party all
around them.

"What about 'Army of the Night'?" Jackie
suggested. "Are we doing the rap part or
not?"

"We've gotta do the rap part," Doland
insisted. "The fans really get into that."

"Yeah," Mike replied. "When we did that
in Houston, we almost had a riot on our
hands."

"A riot? Come on!" Doland mocked.
"A couple of chairs get thrown and you call
that a riot?"

"Some fans got hurt," Mike replied. *"Our*
fans."

Doland threw up his hands. "Nobody got
hurt bad—"

"One girl had to get seventeen stitches in
her forehead. I'd call that bad enough."

Doland fidgeted, barely able to contain his
anger. "Oh, you're such a defender of the
people now, aren't you, Mikey? Next thing
you know, you'll be running for office, man."

Mike shook his head in disgust. He'd had it. "I'm outta here!" He started to leave but turned back. "I just want to know one thing, Doland."

"What's that?"

"Is there *anyone* or *anything* left in this world that you care about . . . besides yourself?"

Mike turned and walked away, barely missing Doland's sly smile. As the door closed, Doland turned to the others and grinned. "Now the party *really* begins."

~

Fifteen minutes later, Scott and Becka's cab arrived at the party site.

"Twenty-two dollars?" Becka gulped.

The cabdriver nodded. "This is L.A., miss. There ain't no place easy to get to."

Becka nodded but didn't completely understand. "Here . . . I'm sorry, I've only got fifty cents left for a tip."

The cabdriver sneered. "Well, ain't this *my* lucky day."

They headed up the walk and rang the bell. Billy Phelps opened the door. "Hey, dudes. C'mon in."

"Do you know where Mike is?" Becka asked.

Billy scratched his head. "He just left. He and Doland had another argument, so he took off. Doland and the guys left right after that."

"Oh no!" Becka said. "We've gotta talk to him!"

Billy shrugged. "Try the hotel."

"I . . . I don't have enough money for a cab."

"Don't worry about it," Billy said. "The other limo is parked in back. Just tell the driver I said it was OK. He'll take you."

Becka smiled. "Thanks, Billy. Let's go, Scotty!"

Scott hesitated. "I'd kinda like to stay here, if it's OK, Beck."

She turned to him, not believing her ears. "After all that happened—you want to stay here?"

Scott shrugged, not able to fully explain why he wanted to stay. He glanced around and lowered his voice to avoid Billy's hearing. "You don't know for certain that those guys were connected with the band."

"I heard them use Doland's name!"

"You probably *thought* you heard them use his name. After all, you were inside that sack getting thrown all around."

"Scotty, who else would've put those guys up to it?!"

"Scott can ride with us to the gig," Billy suddenly said, trying to be helpful. "That way he can help us check everything out."

"C'mon, Beck," Scott pleaded. "This is my last chance to ride with the biggest band in the country. . . ."

Becka wasn't sure what to do. But she knew she had to get to the hotel as fast as she could. "You say Doland's already left?"

Billy nodded.

That gave her some comfort.

"Don't worry, Big Sis," Billy said with a grin. "I'll take care of your little bro."

Becka slowly nodded. "OK . . . but be careful." She ran toward the limo.

∾

As soon as Becka was out of sight, Billy turned to Scott. "So, you want a beer?"

"Uh . . . yeah, sure." Guilt washed over him the minute the words were out of his mouth, but he just clenched his teeth. So what if he was underage? So what if he hated the taste of beer? What he hated even worse was looking like he didn't fit in. Besides, one little beer couldn't hurt, could it?

A few seconds later, Billy had shoved a brew into his hand and headed off, leaving Scott to wander the party, pretending to sip his beer and trying not to look like a geek. He failed in both departments.

It didn't take long to notice that the people at the party were even stranger than the ones at the party after the concert. Nearly all of them were dressed in black. Several had symbols painted on their faces. As Scott walked around, he realized lots of drugs were being passed around.

Scott managed to avoid the occasional joint that was passed through the crowd, but it became clearer by the second that staying had been a mistake. Seeing the plastic skulls, daggers, and pentagrams all over the place didn't help matters either.

He knew that he was taking a risk even being here. But after all he'd been through in the past year, he still sometimes questioned whether having faith in God was worth it. Sometimes having faith was like asking for trouble.

He tried convincing himself to be more open-minded, to pretend that the skulls and daggers were just decorations—like a perpetual Halloween party. That might have worked, too, if he hadn't spotted people in the corner chanting some kind of gobbledygook and others in the kitchen burning black candles and joining hands in a séance.

So much for open-mindedness. He was in way over his head.

Scott searched for Billy to get a ride home. He found him kissing a girl in another room. He felt embarrassed having to interrupt. "Hey, Billy . . ."

"Not now, sport," Billy said without looking up. "Come back later."

Scott backed out of the room, unsure of

how he was going to get out of there. He
decided to see if the limo had returned. But
as soon as he stepped into the backyard, he
sensed that something else was wrong. His
head began to hurt slightly, the way it had in
past demonic encounters. He spotted Jackie
and Grant standing with about a dozen
others near a small bonfire and headed
toward them.

As he approached, he nearly ran into
Doland, who headed up the driveway carry-
ing a small cat. The rocker turned and glared
at him but said nothing. Instead, he continued past him and walked to the center of the
small circle of people.

Scott watched, swallowing back his fear
as Doland raised the squirming cat over
his head and pointed it toward the fire.
The poor animal was in a panic. It wriggled
wildly, desperately trying to get away.

"So, almighty one," Doland called out,
"give to us portions of your power as we
offer this sacrifice to you."

Sacrifice! Doland was about to sacrifice that
poor cat to the devil. Before he could think
about it, Scott shouted, "Stop! What do you
think you're doing?!"

The group turned and stared at him. But
it was Doland's gaze that frightened him the
most. In the glow of the fire, the singer's eyes
seemed to shine. As his body began to shake,

he looked like a wild man . . . like someone
losing control of his will . . . like someone
who had just opened himself up to another
spirit.

Realizing he'd used up all of his courage
with that first shout, Scott silently prayed,
*Dear Jesus, please help me. I've . . . I've really been
stupid. I'm in way over my head. Forgive me for
not praying sooner. Please step in here with your
power.*

Doland shook more violently. Moments
later, Scott's prayer seemed to have an effect
on Doland. He suddenly stopped shaking
and took a step toward Scott.

"You want this cat, freak?" Doland yelled,
holding the wriggling animal above his
head.

Scott nodded. He wanted to speak but
didn't trust his voice.

Doland's smile twisted across his face as
he suddenly hurled the cat at Scott. He managed to get his hands up to prevent his face
from being scratched, but his arms weren't
so lucky. The cat's claws tore into him, draw-
ing blood from three deep cuts.

Scott yelped in pain. Even so, he was glad
to see the cat land safely on the lawn and
bolt into the night. He slowly backed away
from Doland.

Doland continued glaring at him but didn't
come after him. "That's right!" Doland

shouted. "Better get out of here, loser! . . .
Get out while you still can!"

∿

Becka's limo pulled into the big, circular
driveway in front of the hotel. She looked
up in time to see Mike getting into a cab
that started to pull away. She leaped from
the limo and chased the cab down the drive,
shouting and waving her hands. "Stop! Wait
a minute! Mike! Stop!"

But the cab never stopped.

Frustrated, she turned around only to see
the limo she had traveled in pull away as well.
Again she ran, shouting and waving. This
time she was heard. The limo stopped, and
the driver rolled down the window. He was
a kindly looking, gray-haired gentleman.
"Yes, miss?"

Becka tried to catch her breath. "Can . . .
can you take me to the auditorium?"

The limo driver looked at his watch. "I
suppose so, miss. But we'll have to leave right
this moment so I'll have enough time to
swing back and pick up the others from the
party."

Becka looked back toward the hotel. She
wanted to call the suite to have Mom come
down. But there just wasn't time!

With a quick prayer, she climbed back into
the limo. It sped off into the night.

~

Scott held firmly to Billy's jacket as Billy's motorcycle pulled in front of the auditorium.

"Thanks for the ride, Billy!" Scott shouted as he climbed off the bike.

"No problem, man. Listen, I've gotta go in and check some wires. . . . Here's the money you earned working with the crew. I really don't think it'd be a good idea for Doland to see you after what happened at the party. So, you just stay out front, OK?"

Scott nodded. As he took the money, his eyes widened. "Wow! A hundred and fifty bucks! I didn't work enough hours for that!"

"Don't worry. . . . Consider it hazard pay for those cat scratches," he chuckled. "Besides, the other guys on the crew drink up that much just in beer. See you around, Scott."

"See ya, Billy."

~

The lights were off. The hotel room was illuminated only by the flickering flame of the black candle in the center of a table. Doland, the large bald man, and three groupies held hands across the table. The chant began, low at first, but then gradually increasing until it became a shout: "All must die! All must die! All must die!"

And with each word, Doland felt the power within him growing stronger. Tonight would be the night.

10

Becka was one of fifty teenagers crowding around the back-stage door in the auditorium. A huge man with a green beard and a red-dot tattoo in the center of his forehead blocked the entrance. As far as Becka could tell, he only spoke four words: "Not on the list." That's what he said to the girl in front of her and what he said to a dozen others before that.

Becka had had no problem getting inside the auditorium. But the wait at the backstage door was long as one teen after another tried to persuade the guard to let him or her pass.

Each time, he scanned a tiny piece of paper in his hands and said, "Not on the list." Becka guessed that there couldn't have been very many names on the list, since the piece of paper was no larger than a bubble-gum wrapper.

Finally, her turn had arrived. "Hi," she said. "Remember me? I was here the other night for the concert."

The big man showed no sign of recognition.

"I'm Rebecca Williams. I'm a friend of Mike Parsek's."

"Not on the list," the guard said, barely glancing at the paper.

"No," Becka said. "I'm on the list. I'm sure of it. You didn't look close enough. Rebecca Williams."

The guard looked again. "Not on the list."

Becka shook her head, fighting the panic that threatened to wash over her. "No! That can't be right! It's very important that I see Mike before the show. His life may be in danger. Maybe it's under Becka Williams. Look up that name. He calls me that sometimes."

The guard's eyes glazed over.

Becka suddenly felt the girl behind her press against her. "Hurry up, will you?" she muttered. "The man said you're not on the list. So, go already!"

Becka turned around. "This is not what you think. I *am* a friend of Mike's, and he said—"

The girl made a face. "I heard he dumped you."

Becka was shocked. How would this girl know anything about that? "He did not . . . no one dumped anyone. We were just friends and . . . if anyone dumped anyone, it was *I* who did the dumping. . . ."

Again Becka turned back and looked at the guard, hoping that somehow he would remember her.

"Not on the list," he repeated.

∼

Mike stood behind the curtain. The auditorium looked virtually the same as it had for the previous show, except for the more elaborate lighting. One new piece of equipment had been added—an even larger fire cannon.

As Mike strode onto the stage, Billy came out from behind the control board. "So what do you think of her, Mike?" Billy asked, looking at the cannon.

"It's a monster."

"You should see it fire! I tested it earlier today. The fireball went about forty feet up into the rafters. I thought it was gonna blast right through the roof!"

Mike frowned. "What about the crowd? Are we going to be raining fire on them?"

Billy shook his head. "No, it dissolves into nothing after that initial blast. But I'd sure hate to be in that first forty feet. There'd be nothing left but cinders and ash."

Mike nodded, looking slowly along the length of the huge, shiny black barrel. "You're sure this thing is safe?"

"Sure," Billy said. "It's got a warranty and everything. We're gonna fire it off about three times during your solo at half strength and then at full strength at the end like we usually do."

As Mike stared into the large black hole at the end of the barrel, an uneasy feeling swept over him. He shook it off, feeling frustrated. He'd been listening to Rebecca Williams too much.

~

By the time the broadcast had begun, Becka had tried the other five backstage entrances with the same results. In fact, she was pretty sure the guards must be related because they all looked alike and said the same thing.

Except for the last guy. Instead of "Not on

the list," he chose to say "Beat it, bimbo" to every girl and "Beat it, jerk-boy" to every guy.

Finally, the lights dimmed and the music began. With a resigned sigh, Becka searched for her seat.

The crowd was even larger and rowdier than before—for good reason. There were TV cameras everywhere. It was a big event, all right, and the band rose to the occasion.

As Becka made her way to her seat, Doland was already cutting loose in the first song. He was frantic—a madman with a microphone. The crowd hung on his every word.

"Over here! Becka, over here!"

She turned toward the familiar voice and saw Scott waving at her, pointing to the empty seat. "We're over here!" he shouted.

She moved through the crowd toward him, yelling, "I thought you were backstage!"

Scott shrugged as she finally arrived. "Doland showed up at the party and some weird stuff started happening. I'm kinda fired. But Billy gave me a ride over and paid me a hundred and fifty bucks!"

Becka looked at him, caught by one part of what he'd said. "What kind of weird stuff?"

Over the pounding music, Scott explained the intended animal sacrifice and showed her the scratches. "They don't hurt too bad!" he shouted. "Billy poured hydrogen peroxide on them before we took off."

Becka's stomach churned. Something was going to happen. She was certain of it. "I never got to talk to Mike!" she yelled. "Security wouldn't let me pass!"

By now the concert was in full swing. As the TV cameras rolled, The Scream gave the performance of a lifetime. Doland never let up. Jackie Vee's fingers flew over the strings of his guitar as though he were carving an intricate sculpture out of a wall of sound. But it was the rhythm section that really dominated. Mike Parsek was at his peak, pounding out the beat as Grant Simone tracked him lick for lick on the bass.

They were phenomenal, and everyone in the auditorium knew it.

It wasn't until Mike launched into his solo that Becka noticed the new fire cannon. It was huge. But that wasn't what caused her breath to catch. There was something oddly familiar about it. A chill suddenly washed over her. . . .

It was the cannon from her dream.

As Mike increased the pace of his solo, Becka's heart pounded. She had to warn him. Suddenly, a terrible blast shot a huge tongue of fire into the air above the crowd. Everyone screamed, including Becka.

"Take it easy!" Scott shouted to her. "It's all part of the show."

Becka's eyes shot to him. "Not this time, Scotty! This time I think Doland is—"

The sentence was cut off by another mighty blast, even bigger than the last. The crowd screamed as never before, and Mike picked up the pace.

Becka caught sight of Doland as he cheered Mike on from the edge of the stage. One by one the other members of the band left the stage just as they had during the other show. Mike was left to carry on with a fury of drum rhythms.

Becka's eyebrows rose as Doland suddenly slipped behind the curtain. *What's he up to?* she thought. A moment later, she caught a glimpse of him all alone at the control panel. Billy had moved from the panel to watch Mike along with everyone else.

"Scott, let me borrow those binoculars!" Becka shouted. She snatched them and quickly focused on Doland. He was quickly turning a knob on the control panel.

Just like my dream! she thought. Only instead of a gnarled and twisted claw touching the control panel, it was Doland.

Becka began to pray. But when she looked up at the barrel of the cannon, she groaned. It slowly turned toward Mike . . . just as it had in her dream.

Becka bolted, pushing her way through the crowd. She knew she'd never get close enough to warn Mike, but she had to try. *Jesus, Jesus, help me!* she prayed.

Scott moved behind her, trying to help them both navigate through the crowd. But the crowd was wall to wall. No one moved.

"Excuse me! Excuse me, please!" Becka shouted over and over again.

But no one listened.

"Out of the way!" Scott yelled. "This girl's sick! She's going to puke any second! Let us through!"

The crowd instantly parted. Becka and Scott squeezed toward the stage.

Mike neared the peak of his solo. He was so intent on his playing that he didn't even notice the cannon barrel slowly turning toward him.

"Mike!" Becka shouted. "The cannon! The cannon!"

Scott joined in. "The cannon, Mike! Get out of there!"

But it was no use. They could not be heard.

Becka continued pushing through the crowd. The cannon was aimed directly at Mike as he launched into the height of his solo. In just a few moments, it would fire.

"Please, Lord!" Becka prayed out loud now, not caring who heard her. "Save him! Save him!"

Mike feverishly pounded the drums. Becka was so close she could feel the vibrations coming from the cannon as it prepared to ignite.

There were only seconds left. Becka and Scott pushed through the crowd harder and quicker but were still too far from the stage.

They weren't going to make it. She wouldn't be able to warn Mike.

She felt Scott grab her. "Get on my back!" he shouted. "Hurry!"

Scott boosted Becka up to his shoulders. She frantically waved. "Mike! Mike!"

The cannon began to shake.

"MIKE! MIKE!"

And then, suddenly, he looked up and saw her waving.

She pointed frantically toward the cannon.

He turned and saw the barrel pointed his way.

Suddenly, a colossal explosion rocked the stage. Becka screamed, but Mike was already in the air. He leaped off the drum riser, flying through the flames as they ignited his platform, his drums—everything around him.

The crowd screamed as the curtains caught fire. Panic filled the auditorium as fans stampeded toward the exit.

Becka managed to catch a final glimpse of Mike before she tumbled from Scott's shoulders. He staggered to his feet. He looked a little worn and bruised, but he was unhurt.

"Thank you, dear God," Becka prayed as she was jostled this way and that. "Thank you. . . ."

In all of the confusion that followed, Becka and Scott managed to slip by the guard at the backstage door. Once past him, they hurried down the long corridor that ran underneath the stage. When they came out on the other side, they saw Mike helping Billy, Jackie, and Grant clear the instruments and sound equipment away from the charred and smoldering curtain.

"Mike!" Becka shouted as she ran into his waiting arms. They embraced for a long moment.

Finally, Becka pulled away. "I've been trying to warn you for hours!" She swallowed as a sob threatened to choke her voice. "Thank God you're all right." She gave a shaky sigh before continuing, "When two men tried to kidnap me at the hotel, I heard one of them mention Doland's name and something about frying the drummer onstage, and . . . and—" her eyes burned as tears cascaded down her cheeks—"I tried so hard to warn you!"

"You *did* warn me," Mike said softly. He looked deeply into her eyes. "You saved my life!"

Again she embraced him, so happy that he was alive.

"Too bad."

The voice made her grow cold. She turned around to see Doland sneering. "You spoiled the show!" He stalked toward them menacingly. "I wanted to burn you onstage, Mikey. It would've been the best publicity stunt ever. Now, I just get to fire you the normal way."

"You can't fire me," Mike said, his voice trembling slightly.

"And why is that?"

"Because I quit. You're one sick dude, man! I want nothing to do with you or your music!"

"Oh, I'm crushed," Doland sneered. "Lucky for me drummers are a dime a dozen. We can find another one anytime we want."

"Not with me, you won't."

Becka turned to see Jackie stepping forward.

"Or me," Grant said, moving up beside him. "I'm quitting, too. We're all quitting!"

Jackie Vee nodded. "You've gone too far this time, Doland. I think the cops want a word with you now, for what you tried to do to Mike. You're goin' down this time, man."

For a second Doland seemed lost, but only for a second. He spun back around to Becka and Scott, his features suddenly contorting.

Becka braced herself. She had the feeling that something horrible was coming next.

"THIS IS YOUR FAULT!" Doland suddenly growled. His voice was guttural, unearthly. *"YOU ARE THE ONES WHO MUST PAY!"*

The other band members stepped back in alarm as Doland's face contorted until it was unrecognizable.

Becka stood still, watching. This was the hatred she had felt from the moment she first stepped off the shuttle bus at the hotel and caught sight of Doland. Now, waves of hatred bored into her with amazing intensity.

For an instant Doland's face seemed like a grotesque gargoyle mask. She had seen a sudden transformation like that in other encounters.

Doland's face just as suddenly turned back to normal. But she wasn't fooled. She knew the battle was finally out in the open.

As Doland started toward her, she opened her mouth to speak. But nothing came out! Alarm washed over her. She couldn't speak! It wasn't fear—she knew that. She didn't know what it was! Could this be a new power she had never encountered before?

Father, help me! she prayed silently. As she did so, peace washed over her. But still she couldn't speak!

Suddenly, she heard Scott praying softly behind her. "Deliver us from evil, O Lord. Deliver us from evil."

Doland hesitated, shooting Scott an angry

glare. He continued toward them. Soon,
he was only four feet away.

Becka still was held in silence.

Another voice—Mike Parsek's—suddenly
joined Scott's prayer. "Deliver us from evil,
O Lord. Deliver us from evil." His voice was
barely above a whisper.

At that moment, it was as though a gag
were removed. Becka knew that she could
talk once more. Swift understanding came
to her: God had given Mike the opportunity
to step out in faith. And he'd done it! Now
she was allowed to move in and help. She
took a slow, deep breath and spoke clearly:
"In the name of the Lord Jesus Christ, I
command you to stop!"

Instantly, Doland stopped moving.

Becka swallowed, then continued, "I speak
to the demonic force controlling Tommy
Doland." Her voice was stronger now. "In the
name of Jesus Christ and by the power of his
blood, I command you to leave! Come out
from Doland—now! Come out of him and
never enter him again!"

For an instant the gargoyle-like mask
reappeared. But suddenly, Doland's face
returned to normal, as if the demon had
settled back inside of him once more.

"What's going on?" Mike whispered.

Doland grinned and took a step toward
Becka.

"I said come out of him!" Becka ordered. "Come out in the name of Jesus Christ!"

Doland's features changed rapidly in quick succession.

"He doesn't want it to go," Scott explained, with a note of wonder and sadness in his voice.

Becka continued to hold Doland's glare. Despite his hatred and the hideous sneer, she felt sorry for him. Very, very sorry.

Mike looked on, then quietly spoke. "He's condemned himself."

Slowly, sadly, Becka nodded. But there was more work to be done. Her voice broke through the silence, bold and confident. "In the name of Jesus, I command you to leave! Leave and do no more harm to these people!"

Instantly, Doland staggered back. It was as if he were suddenly afraid to even look at them. He retreated another step or two before turning and slinking across the stage.

"Remember," Becka called, "you are bound from ever harming these people again. We command that in the power and authority of Jesus Christ."

All watched in silence as Tommy Doland exited the stage. The police waited for him near the bottom of the stage.

A couple of crew members started to mumble. They'd obviously seen nothing like this before. And, as the encounter faded, Becka felt the weakness return to her body. It was one thing to speak in faith, to feel the power of the Holy Spirit surging through her. But it was quite another to be plain ol' Rebecca Williams.

~

The following day Mike drove Becka, Scott, and Mom to the airport. The four of them had spent most of the night together. By the end of the evening, Mike had not only quit the band but had recommitted his life to Jesus Christ. And, thanks to Mom's gentle urgings, he had even agreed to visit his parents.

"No promises," he said, "but I'll give it another shot."

Now, as they stood at the gate ready to board the plane, Mike turned to Becka one last time. "If it's OK with you, I really *do* want to be your friend."

She looked up at him, swallowing back the tightness growing in her throat.

He continued, "You're one of the few people I know who cares about me because I'm me . . . and not just because I was a member of the hottest band in the country."

She nodded and looked at the ground. It was important that he not see her tears. Saying good-bye was harder than she had expected.

"Oh, and, Scott—" he turned toward her little brother—"I've got something for you." He reached into a small bag and pulled out a Scream T-shirt. "I'm afraid it got a little singed in the fire, but I think you'll like the way it turned out."

He held it up. The shirt was perfectly fine . . . except that one letter was scorched. Where it had once read *Army of the Night,* part of the *N* was burned and smudged. It now read *Army of the Light.*

Scott beamed as he took it. "'Army of the Light.' Now *that's* cool."

A minute later they said their final good-byes. Becka, Scott, and Mom walked down the ramp toward their plane. Becka guessed that Mike would remain to watch their plane take off. Her eyes filled with tears. But they weren't tears of sadness. They were tears of gratitude. She was grateful that they had decided to simply stay friends. But she was even more grateful that once again, Mike Parsek had found, and was getting acquainted with, his very best Friend.

~

On the plane Becka couldn't help but notice that Scott looked more like his old self. "Hey, Scotty, where are the torn jeans?" she teased. "You look halfway normal."

Scott shrugged. "I don't know. I guess I

kind of lost interest in all that stuff. I mean,
I used to think it was, like, really being real.
. . . But there was an awful lot about those
people that wasn't real at all. They used all
that fake booze and stuff just to psych out
the audience."

Mom nodded. "It's kind of strange how
things turned out. At first The Scream and
all of their fans were people I'd want to avoid
like the plague. But if we had, then Mike
might not have returned to his faith."

Scott agreed. "God really does care about
everybody. I guess we can't write anybody off."

"But that doesn't mean we have to be like
them," Becka said, giving him a teasing smile.

"Yeah," Scott sighed as he rubbed his hair,
which still had a touch of yellow and green in
it. "I wonder what the guys on my baseball
team are going to say about this."

In less than two hours the family had
arrived at another airline ramp. Only this
time they were close to home. Becka was the
first to see Ryan at the gate. His jet-black hair
and sparkling smile made him stand out
from the crowd. In one hand he clutched
an envelope, in the other a welcome-home
bouquet of flowers.

Before she knew it, she found herself running through the waiting area to greet him.
As they embraced, she held him tighter than
she had ever held him before. She suddenly

realized how much she had missed him. When they separated, fresh tears sprang to her eyes.

"Hey," he asked in concern, "are you OK?"

She nodded, unable to speak.

"Are you sure?"

She could only roll her eyes. Men . . . would they ever learn?

"Hey, Ryan!" Scott called.

"Hey, Scott. Hi, Mrs. Williams."

"Flowers for me?" Scott joked. "Why, Ryan, you shouldn't have."

"You're right. I shouldn't, and I wouldn't." He faked a punch at Scott and gave the flowers to Becka.

"Ryan . . . they're beautiful." Once again tears welled up in her eyes.

Ryan frowned. "Maybe it's allergies," he said. "You should probably have that looked into."

Before Becka could answer, Scott did what he did best . . . butt in. "What is that?" he asked, motioning to the manila envelope in Ryan's other hand.

"Four tickets to New Mexico. They came in the mail a few days ago," Ryan said. "They're from Z."

"Z?" Becka asked.

Ryan nodded.

"Cool," Scott quipped. "Sounds like another assignment is about to begin."

Becka let out a low, quiet sigh. At that

moment she had had enough of Z's assignments. She just wanted to go home and get some rest.

She was glad when Ryan took her hand as they headed toward baggage claim to pick up their luggage. She had no idea what awaited them in New Mexico—or what spiritual counterfeit she'd have to face next. But for now she was just grateful to be home.

AUTHOR'S NOTE

As I developed this series, I had two equal and opposing concerns. First, I didn't want the reader to be too frightened of the devil. Compared to Jesus Christ, Satan is a wimp. The two aren't even in the same league. Although the supernatural evil in these books is based on a certain amount of fact, it's important to understand the awesome protection Jesus Christ offers to those who have committed their lives to him.

This brings me to my second and somewhat opposing concern: Although the powers of darkness are nothing compared to the power of Jesus Christ and the authority he has given his followers, spiritual warfare is not something we casually stroll into. The situations in these novels are extreme to create suspense and drama. But if you should find yourself involved in something even vaguely similar, don't confront it alone. Find an older, more mature Christian (such as a parent, pastor, or youth leader) to talk to. Let him or her check the situation out to see what's happening. Ask him or her to help you deal with it.

Yes, we have the victory through Christ. But we should never send in inexperienced soldiers to fight the battle.

Oh, and one final note. When this series was conceived, there were really no bad guys on the Internet. Unfortunately that has changed. Today there are plenty of people out there trying to draw young folks into dangerous situations through it. Although the characters in this series trust Z, if you should run into a similar situation, be smart. Anyone can *sound* kind and understanding, but their intentions may be entirely different. All that to say, don't take candy from strangers you see . . . or trust those you don't.

Bill

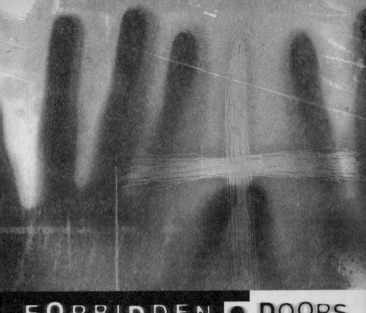

FORBIDDEN ● DOORS

Want to learn more?

Visit Forbiddendoors.com on-line for special features like:

- a really cool movie
- post your own reviews
- info on each story and its characters
- and much more!

Plus—Bill Myers answers your questions! E-mail your questions to the author. Some will get posted—all will be answered by Bill Myers.